The Life I SLEPT INTO

Author:

Mohammad Kaif

Copyright

First Edition, 2025
ISBN: 978-93-5602-614-8
Imprint: MK Publication (Self Published)
Cover & Layout: AtomProd

For permissions or inquiries:
Email: kaif@atomprod.in

Acknowledgments

This book would not exist without the support, belief, and warmth of the people who shaped my journey.

To my family—thank you for filling my life with patience, strength, and the kind of love that grows quietly but lasts loudly. Your encouragement made every word on these pages possible.

To my close friends, who listened to ideas, twists, endings, and rewrites with unwavering enthusiasm—you helped transform a thought into a world.

A heartfelt thanks to everyone who shared their own stories of ambition, struggle, heartbreak, and dreaming. Your experiences breathed life into Omar's.

And finally, to the readers:
Thank you for giving this story a space in your own.

Author's Note

This novel was born from a simple curiosity:
How much of a life can the mind creates while the body sleeps?

In exploring Omar's journey—his victories, heartbreaks, friendships, and losses—I discovered that a dream can hold the same emotional weight as waking reality. The brain does not measure time the way clocks do. It measures attachment, struggle, triumph, fear, and longing.

The line between real and unreal began to blur while writing this book. That is exactly the space I wanted to explore—the border where life feels both lived and imagined.

Omar's story is fictional, but the emotions behind it are deeply human.
We all dream of lives we haven't lived.
We all mourn things that never happened.
We all wake up sometimes with questions that follow us through the day.

This book is my attempt to honour those silent questions.

Thank you for reading.

Introduction / Preface

Twenty-year-old Omar believes he understands the world around him—its limitations, its expectations, its disappointments. Raised in AnuNagari, a small city with big shadows, he steps into adulthood with quiet ambition but no clear path.

One night, after completing his degree and returning home, he falls asleep in the most ordinary way. Nothing unusual happens. Nothing mystical. He simply closes his eyes.

And then he wakes up into another life.

A life that feels real.
A life where seventeen years unfold in vivid detail.
A life where he rises from poverty, builds a groundbreaking company, finds love, loses dreams, creates a family, and ultimately confronts the price of success.

Only at the brink of death does he return to his original timeline—
twenty years old, alive, unchanged physically, but carrying the emotional weight of a lifetime.

This story is not about fantasy.
It is about possibility.
It is about the versions of ourselves that sleep quietly inside us.

And about the question Omar asks at the very end:
Am I still alive

Contents

Chapter 1 – The Last Ordinary Day

The bus left the highway and turned onto the narrower road that led toward **AnuNagari**, its engine groaning as if protesting the decision. A faded yellow board appeared near the roadside, the paint barely holding on:

WELCOME TO ANUNAGARI

No train tracks crossed this land.
They never had.

Anyone traveling here first had to reach **CoachingCity**, fifty kilometres away—a crowded, restless place filled with hostels, classrooms, and ambition. From there, the journey continued by bus or shared jeep, climbing away from noise and opportunity and into quiet containment.

Omar sat on the last seat, his backpack resting between his feet. As the bus rolled past scrubland and low concrete structures, the silhouette of the nuclear facility came into view—tall, distant, and unapproachable. It didn't dominate the skyline; it simply existed, like a reminder no one ever addressed directly.

AnuNagari was built around routine, not growth.

The bus stopped near the market crossing. Omar stepped down, dust settling quickly around his shoes. The sound of the engine faded, leaving behind the soft hum of a town that never raised its voice.

This was home.

BCA. Completed.

The degree certificate lay folded carefully in his bag. It felt heavier than the bag itself.

He adjusted the strap on his shoulder and started walking.

The lanes of AnuNagari were narrow but familiar. Houses stood close together, painted in muted colours that had slowly surrendered to the sun. Clothes dried on wires strung between balconies. A group of children chased a rubber ball, shouting freely, their voices echoing before disappearing into the still air.

Near the main road, the call to prayer rose from the small mosque—measured, unhurried. Omar paused for a moment, listening, then continued walking.

Life here flowed within boundaries.

***

His house stood at the end of a quiet lane, one of many similar structures, built years ago when the town had been planned more than it had been lived in. The main door was open.

“Ammi?” Omar called.

From the kitchen came a familiar response: "Are you here? Leave your bag there. I'm making tea."

He placed his bag near the old cupboard and went to wash his hands. The mirror above the sink reflected a face that hadn’t changed much—sharp eyes, thin frame, the quiet uncertainty of someone who had crossed a milestone without feeling it under his feet.

Twenty years. Nine months.

He stepped into the living area. Sharif Hussain sat on the floor; newspaper open across his lap. He looked up briefly.

“Is the journey still?” his father asked.

“Haan.”

“That’s good.”

No more was needed. In that house, achievements were acknowledged without celebration.

Rehana Bee handed him a cup of tea and sat beside him for a moment. She watched him the way only mothers could—reading more from silence than words.

“What are your plans for the future?” she asked softly.

I took a sip before answering. “Nothing is final yet.”

She nodded. The conversation ended there, not because it lacked importance, but because it carried too much.

***

As evening began pulling shadows across the lanes, Omar stepped out again. AnuNagari didn’t offer many places to go, but routine was comfort.

The open ground beside the **government school** was alive with familiar presence.

Majid Hussain sat on the low boundary wall, phone in his hand, posture loose, unburdened. He had been there since Omar was eight, back

when schoolbags were bigger than problems.

"**Degree-holder sahib**," Majid said, grinning. "What CoachingCity Gives You?"

Omar sat beside him. "Wohi. Certificate aur confusion."

Majid chuckled. "Perfect package."

Moments later, **Hazir Ahmed** arrived, quiet as always. He nodded once and joined them.

"I don't feel like college is over," Hazir said, looking toward the school building. "Like everything is pending."

Omar exhaled slowly. "Nothing ever ends. It just shifts…"

Majid stretched his legs. "It felt the same from private school to government school."

That brought the memory back naturally.

Class three to eight—private school. Promise, pressure, fees. After class eight, reality intervened. Both Omar and Majid shifted to the government school in class nine.

That's where Hazir came in.

Different backgrounds. Same uncertainty.

Together, they learned the art of waiting.

“Next,” Majid said, “do you have to go back to CoachingCity?”

“Maybe,” Omar replied. “There is no work here.”

Hazir studied his face. “You’re not one to shy away from hard work,” he said calmly. “But when you work, you get results. It just takes time for the world to understand.”

Omar didn’t answer.

He already knew that about himself. He just didn’t know if life would allow it.

***

As daylight bled into night, an older memory surfaced quietly.

Shanaya Bee.

Junior. Smiling eyes. Late-night messages that once meant everything. A misunderstanding. A separation without closure.

After class ten, the school itself ended. Higher secondary had brought them under the same roof again—no communication, only passing glances heavy with what could not be said.

After class twelve, she married.

The town absorbed the news the way it absorbed everything else—without surprise.

***

When Omar returned home, dinner was waiting. Conversation was minimal. Fatigue settled into him like dust.

In his room, he lay on the thin mattress staring at the ceiling fan, its rhythm unchanged for years.

No trains passed nearby.
No horns disturbed the night.
Only silence and distant routine.

Tomorrow would arrive whether he was ready or not.

Omar closed his eyes, and slept.

Sleep did not come immediately.

Omar lay on his back, hands resting loosely on his chest, listening to the familiar sounds of the house settling into night. Somewhere outside, a dog barked and then went silent. The ceiling fan continued its uneven rotation, producing a low humming sound that rose and fell like an old breath.

He had slept under this fan for nearly two decades.

The thought should have been comforting. Instead, it made him restless.

His mind wandered—not forward, but backward.

***

When he was younger, life had felt simpler, not because it actually was, but because he had believed intelligence would be enough. Even as a child, Omar had understood things quickly. Concepts made sense to him before teachers finished explaining them. Homework bored him. Revision felt unnecessary.

Adults praised him for it.
"You're sharp," they said.

That sentence followed him everywhere.

A little more effort.
A little more discipline.
A little more seriousness.

What no one ever said was that effort—for him—felt heavier than it seemed to for others. Not because he couldn't do it, but because his mind resisted tasks that didn't excite it. Endless repetition drained him. Long hours dulled him.

Yet when something truly demanded his attention, he moved fast—decisively, almost frighteningly so.

Teachers mistook it for arrogance.
Relatives called it laziness.
Friends learned to accept it.

Majeed used to joke, "One day you will either do something big… or do nothing at all."

Hazir Once said, "You stop too often. But once you start, you don't look back."

Omar didn't know which version of himself would win.

***

A faint clinking sound came from the kitchen.

He turned his head slightly, listening. Rehana Bee was still awake.

The door creaked softly as she entered his room, holding a folded blanket. She moved quietly, careful not to disturb him—or perhaps pretending she hadn't noticed he was awake.

She laid the extra blanket near his feet.

"Can't you sleep?" she asked gently, standing there.

Omar hesitated, then answered honestly. "I will."

She sat down on the edge of the mattress.

For a moment, neither of them spoke.

“College is over,” she said finally, as though testing the words aloud. “Now a new part of life should begin.”

Omar stared at the fan. “Has Life found out?”

She smiled faintly at that, but the smile didn’t last.

“don't take tension,” she said. “Allah opens the way.”

He nodded, not because her words solved anything, but because he wanted to believe them. Rehana Bee reached out and adjusted the blanket near his shoulder, the way she had done since childhood.

“**I'll make an omelette tomorrow morning**." she added casually. “It's been a long time.”

This time, Omar smiled properly.

“**Paratha** bhi,” she said, as she stood up.

“Deal.”

She left the room, switching off the dim light near the door. Darkness settled naturally, not abruptly.

***

Time passed strangely after that.

Omar drifted in and out of half-formed thoughts. Images surfaced and dissolved—classrooms, crowded buses, code running across screens, Majid laughing, Hazir staring out of windows, Shanaya's face appearing briefly and then fading before he could hold it.

He did not dream.

Not yet.

In the other room, Sharif Hussain folded the newspaper he had been pretending to read for the last twenty minutes. He adjusted his spectacles and looked toward Omar's closed door.

"He's Grown up," he said quietly to Rehana Bee.

She nodded. "But still stuck in the middle."

Sharif considered this. "It's not a bad thing to be stuck," he said. "When a man stops, he thinks."

Rehana Bee said nothing. Mothers thought differently. They felt time more urgently.

Sharif stood up, walked to the window, and looked out toward the sleeping town. He had lived his life the way AnuNagari preferred—steady, limited, unquestioning. He wanted better for his son, but not at the cost of breaking him.

"Just don't get lost" hey side softly.

Back in his room, Omar turned onto his side.

Something about the air felt heavier than usual.

Not suffocating—just charged, like the moment before rain when the sky hasn't decided whether to thunder or stay silent. His thoughts had slowed, but they hadn't stopped. They lined up in unexpected ways.

What if nothing changed?

What if CoachingCity was just another detour leading back here—older, more tired, still unsure?

He imagined himself at thirty, still returning by the same bus, still hearing the same azan echo across the town, still sleeping under the same fan.

The image didn't scare him.

That scared him.

A stray thought slipped in, uninvited.

What if this is it?

Not the end—just the shape.

The idea lingered longer than it should have.

His chest felt oddly light, as though something inside him had stepped away from its usual position. He closed his eyes, then opened them again, adjusting to the darkness.

The fan slowed slightly, then resumed its uneven pace.

Omar's breathing steadied.

There was no dramatic transition.

No flash of light.
No falling sensation.
No sense of leaving anything behind.

Just sleep—complete and unresisting.

Somewhere beneath that sleep, time loosened its grip.

The tightly bound rules of effort and reward—the ones he had struggled against all his life—began to blur. Possibility rearranged itself quietly, without announcement.

Not as magic.
Not as fantasy.

Only as permission.

Outside, AnuNagari remained unchanged.

No trains passed.
No roads expanded.
No ambitions announced themselves in neon.

***

The nuclear facility stood in the distance, constant and silent. Houses breathed in unison. The town continued doing what it did best—holding on.

Inside the small room at the end of a narrow lane, a twenty-year-old boy slept under a tired ceiling fan, unaware that he had already stepped into a life that would take him seventeen years to finish.

Still asleep, Omar shifted slightly, his fingers curling inward as if trying to hold onto something invisible. His face remained calm, but beneath that stillness, memories layered themselves quietly—unfinished conversations, unasked questions, roads not taken.

None of them demanded attention. They simply existed, waiting their turn.

The town breathed around him. Somewhere, a late-night cycle passed slowly, its bell ringing once before fading into distance. A generator hummed briefly and then stopped. AnuNagari was good at returning to silence. It had learned that from the things surrounding it—things that required discipline, control, and routine to remain safe.

Omar had grown up absorbing that silence. It had shaped him more than he realized. It taught him to stop before speaking, to think before acting, to wait longer than necessary. Somewhere along the way, waiting had become habit, and habit had begun to resemble surrender.

His breathing deepened, steady and untroubled. In sleep, he did not carry the weight of expectations. He did not owe the world consistency, nor did he owe himself an explanation. Time softened around him, stretching and folding, unbothered by clocks or calendars.

If someone had watched closely, they might have noticed how relaxed he looked—less burdened than he ever appeared while awake. Sleep had removed the question he carried every day: *What now?* For the first time in years, there was no urgency pressing against his chest.

Outside, the wind shifted direction, carrying the distant metallic scent across the town once more. The facility lights glowed faintly against the dark sky, unchanged, dependable. Life continued, structured and unremarkable, unaware that it had just lent one of its own to something far less obedient.

And somewhere in that quiet surrender, without ceremony or announcement, Omar began living the life he had never quite known how to ask for.

***

For a long time, nothing seemed to happen.

Omar's breathing stayed steady; his fingers curled loosely against the thin bedsheet. From the doorway, if anyone had watched, it would have looked like ordinary sleep, the kind that came at the end of tired days and unremarkable years. The ceiling fan kept its uneven pace, blades cutting the air with a soft, repetitive wobble. Shadows from its movement slid across the wall, over the old calendar that still showed a month from three years before.

In the kitchen, the last of the vessels dried in the rack. A small drop of water clung to the edge of a steel glass, then let go, falling soundlessly into the basin. The refrigerator hummed. A lizard stilled itself near the tube light, its chest rising and falling, watching for insects drawn to the glow.

AnuNagari had already practiced the art of being quiet long before Omar was born. Nights here did not sharpen into danger or excitement. They thickened into a dull, even calm. The mosque loudspeaker had gone silent after the last prayer. The main market shutters were down. Even the dogs barked less after midnight, as if they had made an agreement with the town that there was no point in disturbing sleep when nothing urgent ever arrived.

For a while, the quiet inside the room felt almost companion-like—not empty, not heavy, just present. Omar shifted again, turning from one side to the other, adjusting his position as though comfort was something he could negotiate with. Each movement brought a small whisper from the bedsheet, the kind of sound he'd heard thousands of times, yet tonight it seemed louder, sharper, as if the night insisted on reminding him that nothing around him had changed except him.

He let out a slow breath.

The air felt warmer than usual. Or maybe that was inside him.

His gaze drifted toward the faint outline of his study table in the darkness. The books stacked there seemed to blur into one another—subjects he had once understood, memorized, forgotten, relearned, struggled through. They were reminders of a life he had dutifully carried forward, step by step, without ever being certain whether he was walking on a path or merely following a pattern.

One book in particular caught his eye—the worn Java programming guide he had bought second-hand in CoachingCity. He remembered flipping through its pages late at night in his hostel room, not because he enjoyed it, but because he believed he *should*. The idea of success had felt clearer back then. Not easy, but linear—study, effort, opportunity, job. A sequence that teachers preached and students tried to believe in.

But sequences didn't always apply to people like him.

The thought lingered, curling around his mind like smoke.

His mother's earlier words echoed again:
"Allah opens the way."

He wondered if ways opened by themselves or whether people walked blindly until a path accidentally appeared under their feet. Maybe both. Maybe neither. Maybe life wasn't a series of doors but a slow shifting of walls—sometimes closer, sometimes farther, always rearranging themselves just out of reach.

A sudden memory surfaced—one he hadn't thought of in years.

He was eight, sitting outside the same house, holding a broken toy car Sharif had found in the scrap yard. The wheels didn't turn, but Omar had insisted on fixing it. He spent hours examining it from every angle before attempting to push the axle back in place. He didn't succeed, but he remembered how certain he had been that he *would*. That certainty had felt natural then, like breathing.

Where had that confidence gone?

He closed his eyes, letting the memory dissolve.

Another breeze drifted in through the window, carrying with it a faint metallic hint from the facility. A smell he had grown up with. A smell he never questioned. Other towns smelled like rain, dust, markets. His smelled like machinery—subtle but undeniable. He wondered what people in other cities would think of that scent. To him, it was ordinary, the same way all childhood smells became invisible with time.

He turned again, settling on his back, staring into the darkness that seemed to stretch far beyond his room. Somewhere beyond this stillness lay a future he wasn't ready for and a past he couldn't return to. The present felt like a pause—one long, indefinite waiting room where nothing happened but thinking.

A strange calmness washed through him.

Not peace.

Not acceptance.

Just calmness—like the moment after you stop trying to understand something and simply allow it to exist.

His breathing slowed, deepened.

Sleep began seeping through the cracks of his consciousness—first soft, then firmer, then with the steady weight of something inevitable.

As he sank into it, the edges of thought softened, then blended into nothing.

The world outside continued as it always had—unaware, unchanged, unhurried.

And he drifted with it.

There was only one question in Omar's heart: what next?

*****

Chapter 2 – A Morning That Felt Too Clear

Omar woke up before the ceiling fan.

It was an ordinary detail, but it stayed with him—the brief stillness before the fan resumed its uneven rhythm, as though the room itself had waited for him to open his eyes.

Morning light filtered in through the half-curtained window, pale and soft, spreading across the familiar walls. For a moment, he lay still, watching dust move lazily in the air. There was no rush in his body, no heaviness in his limbs. He felt rested in a way that surprised him.

Not refreshed.
Reset.

He sat up slowly.

Everything felt sharper—not brighter, not louder, just clearer. The corners of the room seemed cleaner than they should have been. The cracked paint above the cupboard looked newly washed. Even the faint ache, he usually felt at the base of his neck was gone.

He rubbed his eyes once, firmly, and looked again.

The room remained the same.

From the kitchen came the soft clatter of utensils. Oil sizzled gently. The smell reached him a second later—eggs, familiar and comforting.

“Omar,” his mother called. “Got up?”

“Haan,” he replied, without raising his voice.

He stood, stretched, and felt something unusual—his body responded without resistance. No stiffness. No protest. He washed his face, and the cold water felt more precise on his skin, almost intentional.

In the mirror, his reflection held his gaze a fraction longer than usual. He looked... composed. As if he had already made decisions today that he hadn’t consciously remembered making.

He pushed the thought aside.

***

Breakfast was already on the table when he entered the kitchen.

Omelette.
Paratha.
Tea.

Simple. Warm. Unchanged.

Rehana Bee glanced at him and smiled. “Woke up early today?”

“Looks like I was completely asleep,” he said, sitting down.

Sharif Hussain adjusted his spectacles and folded the newspaper. “What is the plan for the future or is it the same as every day?”

Omar paused—not because he didn’t know the answer, but because the answer arrived quickly. Too quickly.

"I'll go to Coaching City," he said. "I need to see some leads."

Sharif nodded, neutral. “Theek hai.”

No hesitation followed. No internal debate. The decision felt settled the moment it was spoken.

As he ate, Omar noticed something else—time did not drag. Each movement flowed naturally into the next. He finished his breakfast exactly when he felt done, not rushed, not lingering. He stood as his mother reached for the plates, as if they had rehearsed the moment silently.

“I’ll be back by evening,” he said.

“Check bus times,” Rehana Bee replied.

“Haan.”

He picked up his wallet, phone, and bag, checking them without anxiety. Everything was where it should be. Even the small tear in the strap of his bag—something that usually annoyed him—didn’t register as a problem.

He stepped outside.

The street looked the same, yet different.

Not in appearance, but in behaviour. A man crossing the road did so just as Omar reached the corner. A shop shutter lifted the moment he approached. The shared jeep heading out of town slowed down slightly, giving him enough time to wave it down without breaking into a run.

Coincidence, he told himself.

He climbed in and sat by the window.

As the vehicle pulled away from AnuNagari, Omar watched the town recede—low buildings, quiet lanes, routine preserved. His mind, however, had begun moving ahead already.

Job listings.
People to call.
A general sense that today would yield something.

This wasn't hope. Hope usually came with tension.

This was certainty—quiet, unforced.

Halfway to CoachingCity, his phone buzzed.

A message from Majid.

"Will you go to Coaching City today?

Omar typed back: **"Haan."**

Three dots appeared, disappeared.

"Call me later."

"Nahi," Omar replied, then added, **"We will meet in the evening."**

He locked the phone without overthinking it. Strangely, he already knew how the day would move—not in detail, but in direction. Like remembering a route, he hadn't walked in years.

***

CoachingCity announced itself before it appeared.

Noise rose first.
Horns, engines, voices competing with one another.
Then buildings—closer, taller, impatient.

This was where people came to become something else.

Omar stepped out near the bus stand, blending into the crowd instantly. No hesitation. No second-guessing. He began walking, phone in hand, scrolling through saved contacts and notes.

A number caught his eye—an old senior from college. Someone he had avoided calling before, unsure of what to say.

This time, he dialled without pause.

The call connected after two rings.

"Hello?"

"It's Omar," he said evenly. "We spoke once after finals."

A brief silence. Then recognition. "Yah, I know, say"

"I'm in CoachingCity today," Omar said. "Wanted to meet. Talk about work."

Another pause—shorter this time.

"Okay. You came today??" the voice asked.

"Haan."

"Come by the office. I'll be free in an hour."

"Perfect."

Omar ended the call and stood there for a moment, the city moving around him. The exchange replayed in his mind—not for doubt, but for curiosity.

He hadn't planned this call last night.
He hadn't rehearsed it.

It had simply happened.

And it worked.

As he began walking toward the address, Omar felt the smallest flicker of unease.

Not fear.

Awareness.

Life had never responded to him this way before—not this smoothly. He was used to obstacles, to friction, to effort required simply to be noticed.

Today felt like the opposite.

As if resistance had been quietly removed.

He slowed his pace slightly, observing his own thoughts.

They were orderly. Focused. Free of noise.

For the first time in a long while, Omar wasn't waiting for life to decide something for him.

He was already moving.

***

The office was tucked above a row of photocopy shops and snack stalls, the kind of building that tried to look professional by painting its walls white and keeping the reception quiet. Omar climbed the narrow staircase slowly, not out of hesitation, but because he felt no urgency. His body moved at a pace that felt exactly right.

At the door, he paused briefly, then pushed it open.

Air conditioning met him immediately. The room was modest—rows of desks, a few computers, a glass cabin toward the back. Nothing impressive. Nothing intimidating. He had imagined this moment before, usually with his chest tightening and his thoughts scrambling to keep up.

That did not happen.

A receptionist glanced up. "You're here to see Arvind?"

Omar nodded. "Yes."

She gestured toward a chair. "He'll be free in a few minutes."

Omar sat. Instead of reaching for his phone, he leaned back and observed the room. People moved with familiar urgency—typing, answering calls, glancing at clocks. He felt strangely separate from it, like someone watching a system from the outside for the first time.

When Arvind stepped out, he recognized Omar immediately.

"You came faster than I expected," he said, smiling. "Come in."

Inside the cabin, the conversation unfolded easily. Too easily.

Arvind spoke about projects, about clients, about how fresh graduates struggled to adapt to real-world problems. Omar listened, nodding at the right moments. When asked questions, his answers came without effort—clear, structured, confident.

He did not oversell himself.
He did not underplay either.

At one point, Arvind leaned back in his chair, studying him.

"You think differently," he said. "Not aggressively. More like... efficiently."

Omar acknowledged this without pride.

They discussed a short-term contract. Nothing glamorous. But when Arvind mentioned a technical challenge, their team had been unable to streamline, Omar asked a few questions—precise ones. Then, slowly, he described an approach. Not as a solution, just as a possibility.

The room went quiet.

Arvind turned toward his screen, pulled up a relevant file, ran through the data. His fingers moved slowly at first, then faster.

After a minute, he stopped.

"That actually reduces the workload by half," he said, disbelief evident in his voice.

Omar waited.

"How long would it take you to build this?" Arvind asked.

"Two days," Omar replied after a brief pause. "Maybe less."

Not showing off. Just stating fact.

Another silence followed.

"All right," Arvind said finally. "Let's do this. I'll pay you for the prototype. If it works, we talk long-term."

They shook hands.

Omar stepped out to the office less than an hour after he had entered it.

The world outside looked unchanged. The same shops. The same noise. The same crowds moving with inherited urgency.

Yet Omar stood there, oddly still.

He had not struggled.
He had not convinced.
He had not doubted.

Something inside him shifted—not excitement, not joy—but recognition.

***

He walked without destination for a while, letting CoachingCity surround him. Students passed by with backpacks heavier than their posture. Coaching center banners advertised futures with mathematical certainty. Parents waited near hostels, faces tense with hope.

Omar had been one of them once—absorbing pressure quietly, promising himself that clarity would come later.

Later had arrived without announcement.

He took out his phone and called Majid.

When Majid picked up, Omar spoke first. “Found something.”

A brief pause. “Already?”

“Yes.”

Majid laughed lightly. “That was fast.”

Omar smiled. “I know.”

They agreed to meet in the evening. The call ended.

As he put the phone away, a question surfaced gently in his mind.

Why wasn’t he surprised?

He spent the afternoon at a small café, working on his laptop. The code flowed. Blocks aligned naturally, as if he were correcting something that already existed instead of creating it. Time behaved differently around him—hours compressed without strain.

When he finally leaned back, stretching his arms, the screen displayed a clean, working model.

Two days of work. Finished in one afternoon.

That should have alarmed him.

Instead, he felt... settled.

He sent the files. Closed the laptop. Paid the bill.

As evening approached, Omar walked toward the bus stand. The bus back to AnuNagari was already there, engine running patiently. He boarded without hurry and found a window seat.

The city pulled away gradually, its noise dissolving as buildings thinned and lights spaced themselves farther apart.

That was when the doubt finally appeared.

Not fear.
Not suspicion.

Just a mild, unsettling disparity.

Things had always required pushing before. Even his small successes came with resistance—delays, rejections, exhaustion. Today had offered none of that. Every door he approached had opened at the exact moment he reached for it.

He replayed the day in his mind carefully.

Nothing impossible had happened.
No dramatic coincidence.
No sudden miracle.

Just alignment.

And that, somehow, felt unfamiliar.

***

The bus crossed into AnuNagari as the sky darkened. The outline of the nuclear facility appeared briefly against the horizon; its presence as steady as memory.

Home felt closer than usual.

When he entered the house, his mother was in the kitchen, and his father sat in his usual spot. They looked up as Omar stepped in.

“You’re back early,” Rehana Bee said.

“Work finished quicker than expected,” Omar replied, surprised to find the words true.

He ate dinner quietly, answering questions simply. No grand announcements. No explanations. He himself did not fully understand what he was announcing.

***

They met where they always met—by the low wall that edged the government school, the same cracked concrete that had held their weight through board exams, petty fights, and long talks. Night had drawn a cool veil across AnuNagari; the air smelled of dust and frying oil, of distant jasmine and late diesel. Lanterns guttered in a nearby lane, throwing long, lazy shadows that seemed to make time itself slower.

Majid was there first, perched like a bird on the wall, phone dim beside him. Hazir arrived a few minutes later, walking with the steady, unhurried gait that made him look older than he was. They greeted Omar in the way that needed no ceremony—two quick daps, a shoulder bump, an easy smile.

“You look different,” Majid said before the customary chatter began. “Today you’re... sorted.”

Omar shrugged, settling down beside them. “Maybe the day did the work for me.”

Majid laughed, the sound bright in the stillness. “Careful. If days start working for you, they’ll expect payment in glory.”

Hazir watched him with that patient look of his. “So, what happened today? You went to CoachingCity, met an uncle who gave you a job?”

“No uncle,” Omar said. “Just met an old senior. Arvind. He gave me a short contract—prototype work. If it works, maybe longer.”

Majid’s eyes widened. “So, you’re a contractor now? Big man.”

“I’m not a man yet,” Omar said, smiling despite himself. “Just someone who fixed a technical bottleneck in a few hours.”

“Fixing a bottleneck,” Hazir repeated. “You always make problems look small.”

“It’s not that,” Omar said, looking at his hands as if they suddenly belonged to someone else. “It was easy. Too easy. That’s the strange part.”

Majid whistled softly. “So, the universe finally noticed you. About time. Maybe it was waiting for you to be less dramatic.”

Omar leaned back on the wall, letting the evening press against his shoulders. The town around them continued its small, repeating rituals—women returning from late chores, an old man sweeping his threshold, the distant lull of a television drama. The ordinariness comforted him, anchored him. Still, an unfamiliar thread of certainty tugged at his thoughts.

"I felt like doors opened when I reached them," he said. "Not in some mystical way—just... the right things happened when I asked."

Hazir nodded slowly. "Luck Favors the prepared."

"That's what they tell us," Majid said. "But you prepared by not preparing. That's your trick."

"It's not trickery," Omar replied. "It's... I don't know. Focused work. I moved quickly when asked. It felt like fixing something that was already half-made."

They let the idea rest between them. Majid picked at a loose thread on his shirt, eyes roaming the empty schoolyard.

***

Later, in his room, he lay down again beneath the ceiling fan.

The same fan.
The same room.

Yet something fundamental had shifted.

As he closed his eyes, his thoughts did not scatter as they usually did. They aligned, one after another, like markings on a ruler.

Tomorrow already felt decided.

And for the first time in his life, Omar wondered—not with fear, but with calm curiosity—what it would feel like if life continued responding this way.

*****

Chapter 3 – Hyderabad for Twelve Thousand

The job offer arrived without drama.

There was no official appointment letter at first—just a call, brief and direct, from a human resources executive whose tone suggested she repeated the same sentences several times a day. She mentioned the salary almost apologetically, as though she expected resistance that never came.

Twelve thousand per month.

Omar did not negotiate.
He did not hesitate.
He simply accepted.

Because at that point in his life, the number itself mattered less than what it represented: movement.

Hyderabad was not spoken about much in AnuNagari. It existed only as a name—distant, large, detached from anything familiar. People went to CoachingCity to study, to struggle, to return disillusioned.

Hyderabad was where people went to disappear into work.

That appealed to Omar.

He packed lightly. Two changes of clothes, his laptop, a notebook he barely used, and a phone charger with a broken wire that still worked if bent at the right angle. His mother silently added folded rotis wrapped in cloth, even though the journey would take less than a day.

“Keep phone charge,” she said.

“Haan,” he replied.

His father stood at the door; hands clasped behind his back. “Work will hard,” he said carefully, as though stating a weather condition.

“I know,” Omar said.

Sharif Hussain nodded once. “You're going to learn. Remember this.”

Omar didn’t argue with that either.

The bus took him to CoachingCity before dawn. From there, the train carried him south, cutting through regions Omar had never seen before. The land changed slowly—roads widened, stations grew louder, signs appeared in unfamiliar scripts. He watched it all pass with the mild curiosity of someone who did not fully belong to the place he was leaving, nor the one he was entering.

When the train arrived in Hyderabad, the platform exploded into sound.

Announcements overlapped. Vendors shouted. People walked with purpose, not looking around, not slowing down. Omar stepped off with his backpack and stood still for a moment, letting the city register him before he registered it.

The air smelled different.
Heavier. More urgent.

This was not a place that waited.

***

The first problem appeared immediately.

Accommodation.

He had delayed thinking about it, fully aware that it would be an issue but unwilling to let that stop him. Hostels were full. Paying guest rooms demanded deposits he did not have. Shared apartments required references, stability, assurances.

Omar had none of those.

By evening, he found himself sitting on a bench near the railway station, watching people come and go with bags larger than his life plans. Hunger crept in slowly, not painfully, just insistently. He bought a plate of rice from a stall and ate standing up.

Night fell faster than he expected.

He checked his phone. Messages from Majid and Hazir waited, casual but concerned.

"Reached?"
"Settled?"

Omar typed back with careful neutrality. "Reached. Work starts tomorrow."

He did not mention the bench.
He did not mention that he had nowhere to sleep.

The idea occurred to him without panic. The railway platform was crowded, but not hostile. He had seen people sleep there before. Entire families. Workers between shifts. Students waiting for trains that arrived at unreasonable hours.

He adjusted his backpack to use as a pillow and chose a corner where the light was dimmer.

The floor was cold. The noise persistent. But his body did not resist as much as his pride expected it to. He lay down, staring at the ceiling beams, watching shadows move as trains arrived and departed.

This, he noted calmly, was not a tragedy.

It was a phase.

***

The office was located in an aging IT park on the outskirts of the city. The building had the appearance of something that had been important once and then naturally outgrown. Inside, desks were arranged without logic, wires ran where they found space, and deadlines moved faster than understanding.

Omar arrived early on his first day.

He always did—not out of discipline, but because arriving late created questions he preferred not to answer.

The work itself was immediately familiar. Systems that had grown inefficient through neglect. Code that worked but did not think. Processes that assumed human fatigue as default.

He observed quietly.

Others stayed late, eyes strained, fingers heavy on keyboards. Omar finished his assigned tasks in half the time and then stopped. He did not ask for more. He waited.

This confused his teammates.

By the end of the week, someone commented on it.

“You leave right on time,” a colleague said, not accusingly, but with curiosity.

“I finish,” Omar replied.

That was the truth.

During lunch breaks, he ate sparingly. Savings needed to stretch. Even then, the arithmetic worked out poorly. Twelve thousand barely covered food, transport, and occasional internet access. Rent was out of the question.

Some nights, he slept at the railway station. Other nights, on the floor of a colleague’s room when offered. He carried his toothbrush everywhere.

He did not resent it.

What unsettled him slightly was how little effort he felt it took to endure this.

***

As days turned into weeks, patterns emerged.

His manager noticed his output but misunderstood the cause. He assumed Omar worked after hours, unseen. He praised his dedication during meetings.

Omar never corrected him.

There was a room in the office used rarely, filled with outdated monitors and unused servers. On quiet afternoons, Omar sat there, experimenting. He rewrote portions of the system. Simplified things others had added complexity to.

What took teams days took him hours.

Not because he tried harder—because he did not.

He removed what was unnecessary.

That became his habit.

One evening, as he walked back toward the station, the city lights reflecting off puddles left by a recent rain, the thought surfaced uninvited.

If this is what work is, why is everyone so exhausted?

The answer came immediately.

They were working against the system. He was slipping through it.

On a Sunday afternoon, while sitting near the platform yet again, Omar watched a young boy sleeping beside his parents, his head cradled by his mother's arm. The child breathed easily, untroubled by the noise.

The scene reminded him of AnuNagari. Of silence disguised as routine.

Here, stillness had to be found deliberately.

He checked his account balance. Low, but steady.

He could leave.

The thought surprised him.

Not because he wanted to, but because the option felt available. For the first time, he was not trapped by circumstances—only by choices he had not yet made.

His phone buzzed.

A message from an unfamiliar number.

It was his manager.

“We need to talk tomorrow. There’s an issue you might be able to solve.”

Omar stared at the screen, then looked up at the station ceiling.

He felt no anxiety.

Only anticipation.

***

That night, lying on the hard floor of the platform, backpack under his head, Omar watched the lights flicker as trains passed. His body accepted the discomfort without protest. His mind, however, was active—not restless, but alert.

Something about this life—this version of struggle—felt provisional. As though it existed only to introduce him to something larger.

He closed his eyes, not to escape, but to rest.

Around him, the city continued its relentless movement. People arrived. People left. Announcements repeated.

And somewhere in the quiet alignment between his effort and outcome, Omar began understanding that hardship did not always demand suffering.

Sometimes, it simply demanded direction.

The meeting did not begin with urgency.

Omar noticed that immediately.

His manager, Suresh, closed the cabin door with more care than necessary and gestured for Omar to sit. The glass walls dulled the noise of the office into a distant murmur. For a moment, Suresh simply adjusted papers on his desk, as though trying to decide how to begin.

“There’s a module,” he said at last, looking up. “Legacy code. Nobody wants to touch it.”

Omar nodded. He had already guessed as much.

“It breaks every time we scale traffic,” Suresh continued. “We’ve added patches, temporary fixes, extra people. Nothing holds.”

“What do you want it to do?” Omar asked.

Suresh blinked. “Work,” he said. Then corrected himself. “I mean—work without babysitting.”

Omar leaned back slightly. “Then stop patching it.”

There was no disrespect in the tone. Just clarity.

Suresh frowned. “It’s been written over ten years. Rewriting means risk.”

“Keeping it means certainty,” Omar replied.

The words hung between them.

Suresh exhaled. “Can you take a look?”

Omar nodded once. “I already have.”

That surprised even him.

Suresh opened his mouth to ask more, then closed it again, opting instead to turn his monitor so Omar could see. They walked through the code together. Suresh pointed out points of failure; Omar listened, then began suggesting removals.

Not optimizations. Eliminations.

By mid-afternoon, Omar was working out of the unused server room again, keys tapping in a rhythm that felt natural. He ignored the lunch break. Hunger was present but unimportant.

The code resisted briefly, then yielded.

By evening, the system stabilized under simulated load.

Suresh stood beside Omar’s screen, arms crossed, staring.

“This would have taken the team weeks,” he said.

Omar shrugged. “They were trying to save everything.”

“Are you saying we built it wrong?”

“No,” Omar said. “Just that you kept building on the wrong parts.”

That night, Omar did not go to the railway station.

A colleague offered him the floor of his room again, insisting more firmly this time. Omar accepted—not out of desperation, but because refusing would have required explanation.

He lay under a rotating fan that night, staring at a ceiling unfamiliar enough to keep him awake. Yet his thoughts were calm.

He was not proud.

Pride implied arrival.

This felt like calibration.

***

The following weeks rearranged themselves around Omar.

Not visibly, not suddenly—but unmistakably.

More work came his way, though never officially reassigned. People began asking him questions quietly, away from meetings. He answered efficiently and returned to his tasks. He no longer stayed unnoticed, but attention still slid off him easily; he neither sought it nor resisted it.

His manager advocated for him indirectly, referencing “efficiency” and “initiative” during reviews. The salary remained unchanged. Titles did not appear.

That was acceptable.

Because Omar had begun observing something else.

Effort no longer matched outcome.

Others worked longer hours, grew tired, celebrated small victories loudly. Omar worked less, solved larger problems, and went back to waiting.

This imbalance did not make him arrogant.

It made him curious.

One night, back on the platform—because money still required obedience—he sat upright instead of lying down. A train thundered past, sending warm wind across his face.

Twelve thousand.

He tried to imagine spending the next five years at that number.

The image felt illogical.

Not because he felt he “deserved” more—but because the current arrangement wasted something. Like forcing a machine to run at one-quarter capacity while praising its endurance.

He opened his notebook, the one he rarely used, and wrote two lines.

What is actually valuable here?
What can be separated and rebuilt?

He did not know yet how to answer them.

But the questions felt correct.

On a late evening, after finishing another task ahead of deadline, Omar found his manager waiting near his desk.

“Walk?” Suresh asked.

They stepped outside. The air had cooled. Streetlights buzzed faintly.

“You’re leaving money on the table,” Suresh said suddenly.

Omar did not reply immediately.

“You could push,” Suresh continued. “Ask for a raise. A team. Visibility.”

“And then?” Omar asked.

Suresh considered. “Then you move up.”

Omar nodded slowly. “I don’t want to move up inside this.”

That earned him a long look.

“What do you want, then?”

Omar thought about it. The answer arrived without conflict.

“Control,” he said. “Over what I build. And over how much effort it needs.”

Suresh smiled—not mockingly, but with understanding. “That’s dangerous.”

“Yes,” Omar agreed.

They walked back in silence.

That night, Omar slept without dreams.

***

Weeks later, something shifted.

The company lost a client abruptly. Tension spread across the workplace like a thin crack through glass. Meetings multiplied. Decisions slowed. Panic crept in carefully dressed as planning.

Omar watched without participating.

When asked to propose solutions, he spoke briefly. Remove dependencies. Simplify deliverables. Focus on what scaled naturally.

Few listened.

Then came the layoffs.

Two desks near him were emptied by noon. The atmosphere changed. Survival replaced ambition.

Omar was not called into the meeting.

That was when he understood: stability was accidental here.

That evening, he withdrew a portion of his savings and booked a return train ticket—not to AnuNagari, but to CoachingCity.

Not to escape.

To reset.

At the platform, waiting with his bag at his feet, Omar watched people hurry past, carrying destinations like obligations.

He did not feel anxious. He felt finished.

Hyderabad had done its work.

Not by rewarding him—but by revealing limits.

The train arrived late. He boarded, found a window seat, and watched the city stretch and shrink as the wheels turned north.

He thought of Majid. Hazir. Of the quiet certainty with which they accepted life as it arrived.

He thought of AnuNagari—routine, silence, expectation.

And for the first time, those thoughts did not pull him backward. They aligned.

***

By the time the train slowed near CoachingCity, Omar had made a private decision.

He would not search for another twelve-thousand job.

Not here. Not anywhere.

He did not know yet what would replace it. He only knew that he would not trade speed, clarity, and control for endurance again.

As the platform came into view, crowded and familiar, Omar stood and lifted his bag.

***

As the platform came into view, crowded and familiar, Omar stood and lifted his bag. The train hissed, slowing with a long metallic sigh, as though relieved to return him to a place that understood him better than the city he had just left behind.

When the train finally stopped, passengers surged forward in their usual rush, but Omar didn't rush with them. He stepped down quietly, letting the swarm move past him. CoachingCity's noise wrapped around him instantly—buses honking, vendors shouting, parents bargaining with auto drivers, students weaving through crowds with bags overloaded with dreams and fear.

He walked slowly toward the exit, his mind unusually calm for someone who had just abandoned a job without a backup plan. If anything, the lack of panic surprised him. Normally, uncertainty pressed against his ribs like a tight hand. Today, it rested nearby like a silent companion.

Outside the station, heat rose from the ground in soft waves, carrying with it the familiar smells of fried snacks, dust, and printed paper. CoachingCity looked exactly as it had the first day he arrived years ago—alive, frantic, overflowing with intent. Yet it felt different now, not because the city had changed, but because he had.

He adjusted his bag on his shoulder and walked toward the street where hostels lined up like mismatched dominoes. Students hung from balconies, books in their hands, anxiety in their eyes. Coaching center hoardings loomed overhead, each one shouting promises.

Become an engineer.
Become a doctor.
Become someone.

He had once believed those billboards spoke to him. Now he only saw them as background noise in a place too busy to question its direction.

Halfway down the street, he paused near a tea stall. The vendor, a man with a stained apron and a permanent tired smile, nodded in recognition.

"City se aaye?" he asked.

Omar nodded. "Haan. Ek chai."

The vendor handed him a glass within seconds. Omar took a sip. It was strong, hot, sweet—exactly the taste of every uncertain turning point he had lived here.

As he sipped the tea, he watched a group of boys nearby discussing test results, comparing marks, forecasting futures with a seriousness that did not belong on their young faces. One looked terrified, another overconfident, a third pretending not to care.

Omar recognized all three versions. He had been each one at different times.

He finished his tea, set the glass down, and walked further into the city. The narrow lanes gradually widened, leading toward the part of CoachingCity where small offices and freelance studios operated in cramped buildings. He didn't know exactly where he was going, but his feet moved with the sense that direction mattered more than destination.

For a brief moment, doubt surfaced—quiet but distinct.

What if this is a mistake? What if I misread the signs? What if Hyderabad was the only chance?

But the doubt dissolved just as quickly, unable to anchor itself.

Because deep beneath the uncertainty, something clearer had taken root: a growing understanding that the world did not reward endurance alone. It rewarded clarity, precision, timing. Hyderabad had shown him his threshold; CoachingCity would show him his beginning.

He stopped near a small intersection where wires tangled overhead like restless thoughts. Auto rickshaws zipped past, each one offering a different route, a different possibility.

He didn't flag any of them.

Instead, he tightened the grip on his bag, breathed once, and continued walking into the city—not because he knew what came next, but because for the first time, he wasn't afraid not to know.

This was not a return.

This was a reset.

And resets, he understood now, didn't require a plan. They required movement.

He kept walking.

This was not an ending.

It was a refusal.

And in that refusal, something else—unnamed but undeniable—began preparing to take shape.

*****

Chapter 4 – Lazy, But Not Small-Minded

CoachingCity had a way of shrinking people or sharpening them.

It did both at once, often without warning.

Omar stepped off the train just after dawn, blending immediately into the movement of bodies that flowed across the platform. Students moved with rigid purpose, backpacks heavy, eyes fixed ahead as though slowing down might cost them something invisible but essential. Vendors shouted offers without emotion. Engines hummed. Announcements echoed half-finished sentences.

This was not a city that listened.

It demanded.

Omar adjusted the strap of his bag and walked out without hesitation. Unlike his earlier visits years ago, when uncertainty had made every step deliberate, this time his movements felt aligned. He did not rush, but he did not linger either. The city met him without resistance, as if recognizing something it could work with.

He did not come back to CoachingCity for a job.

That thought crystallized clearly as he crossed the road outside the station.

In the past, his stays had been shaped by waiting—waiting for results, for calls, for outcomes dictated by someone else's schedule. Hyderabad had stripped that patience down to its bones. He had seen what endurance paid and what it did not. More importantly, he had understood what kind of endurance exhausted him and what kind empowered him.

He could last.

But he could not repeat.

***

He found a cheap lodge near the older education district, the kind that survived purely due to turnover. The room was small, the fan aggressive, the mattress thin. It accepted daily rent. That mattered more than comfort.

After dropping his bag, Omar sat on the edge of the bed and opened his laptop.

Not to apply.

To observe.

He revisited the notes he had scribbled during those last nights in Hyderabad. Two lines stared back at him, uncomplicated and unwilling to disappear.

What is actually valuable here?
What can be separated and rebuilt?

He had seen systems fail not because of lack of effort, but because of accumulated complexity. Everyone kept adding. Nobody removed.

This city thrived on addition. Coaching. Modules. Content. Metrics. Motivation. Layers upon layers, promising certainty.

Omar suspected that clarity itself might be the rarest product here.

He spent the morning walking.

Not searching for opportunity—mapping tension.

He passed giant coaching institutes and smaller, nameless buildings where the real work often happened silently. He studied the rhythm of the city: when traffic thickened, when students spilled out in clusters, when chai stalls transformed from pit stops into confessionals.

Everyone was striving toward something measurable.

Ranks.
Offers.
Salaries.
Admits.

Failure here was not poverty; it was irrelevance.

That was why the city worked.

By noon, Omar found himself seated at a roadside stall, notebook open, pen uncapped. He watched names being written on forms. Fees calculated. Deadlines circled.

Too much dependency, he thought.
Too much human fatigue.

He did not write an idea.

He wrote observations.

***

By afternoon, the familiar discomfort of idleness crept in—not impatience, but expectation. This was the state that usually preceded avoidance in him. The moment when effort demanded engagement without clarity. In the past, he had distracted himself then.

Now, he leaned into it.

Back in the lodge, he opened a fresh document and began dismantling something he knew well: the way people used technology when pressure was high.

Most systems treated users as diligent. CoachingCity proved otherwise.

People did not want more effort. They wanted friction removed.

Omar moved fast, not because he was excited, but because the structure formed itself cleanly in his mind. Screens became simpler. Decision trees collapsed. He erased entire sections without regret.

By evening, he had the rough foundation of something—not a product, not yet, but an approach.

That night, while stepping out for food, his phone buzzed.

A familiar name appeared.

Kabir Mehta.

They had known each other during college—not closely, but well enough to speak honestly. Kabir had been louder, sharper at the edges, unafraid to pitch ideas aloud even when most of them went nowhere.

Omar answered.

“You’re back in CoachingCity?” Kabir asked.

“Yes.”

“Good. Then you owe me tea.”

Omar smiled slightly. “Where?”

Kabir named a place without pause.

***

Kabir arrived late, unapologetic.

He dropped into the chair opposite Omar and launched into a half-finished monologue about contracts, freelancing headaches, and how everything ambitious felt one setback away from collapse.

Omar listened.

At some point, Kabir stopped talking and frowned.

“You’ve changed,” he said. “You’re not dodging the problem anymore.”

Omar took a sip of tea. “I got tired of repeating it.”

“That’s dangerous.”

“Yes.”

Kabir grinned. “I like dangerous.”

They talked until the stall owner began stacking chairs.

Kabir spoke about demand. Omar spoke about waste. Their ideas did not match at first—but they did not repel either.

At the end, Kabir leaned back and studied him.

"You're not looking for a job," he said. "No."

"You're not scared either."

Omar considered this. "No."

Kabir smiled. "Then we're already ahead of most people here."

When Omar returned to his room that night, he did not feel the exhaustion he typically associated with progress. His mind remained active, but not scattered.

For the first time, his laziness was not resistance.

It was selectivity.

He would work hard at removing effort.

Sleep came easily.

And beneath it, the shape of something uncomfortably precise began to form.

Not ambition.

Direction.

***

The idea did not arrive fully formed.

It never did.

What Omar carried back to the lodge that night was not an invention but a pressure—an irritation with how systems demanded effort where intelligence could remove it. He lay on the narrow bed, staring at the ceiling fan cutting uneven circles through warm air, replaying Kabir's words and his own silences.

Removing effort can scale, he thought.
If you remove it in the right place.

In Hyderabad, he had removed effort from code.
In CoachingCity, effort lived elsewhere.

In confusion.
In repetition.
In interfaces designed to look important rather than work cleanly.

The next morning, he did not open his laptop immediately. He showered, ate minimally, then walked. He needed friction—human friction—to test where pressure collected.

He spent hours inside coaching institutes pretending to ask for information. He watched counsellors repeat explanations. He saw students struggle not with concepts, but with navigation—schedules, portals, updates, progress tracking.

Technology existed everywhere.

Usability did not.

By the time he returned to the lodge, clarity had replaced irritation.

He opened his laptop.

And worked.

***

Over the next several days, Omar and Kabir met intermittently—not daily, not scheduled. Kabir was the opposite of Omar in rhythm.

He burst with urgency, spoke in projections, chased momentum. Omar waited, observed, then cut.

At first, this created friction.

“You can’t keep removing everything,” Kabir argued one afternoon, pacing the room. “People like features. They need to feel something is happening.”

“They need results,” Omar replied calmly. “Features are noise.”

Kabir stopped pacing. “Noise sells.”

“Only once,” Omar said. “Silence retains.”

That line stayed between them longer than either expected.

They argued over architecture, presentation, timing. Kabir wanted speed. Omar wanted clarity. Somewhere between those impulses, something stable emerged.

They named it without ceremony.

Nuclear Technologies.

Kabir suggested the name half-jokingly, half-provocatively. Omar did not smile—but he did not reject it either.

“It fits,” Omar said after a moment. “Controlled energy. Massive impact. Minimal waste.”

Kabir nodded slowly. “And dangerous if misused.”

“Exactly.”

The company did not exist yet.

But the name settled in place like it always had.

***

They registered a simple domain. No expensive branding. No extensive pitch decks. The work mattered more than how it looked—at least, that was Omar’s position. Kabir compromised by insisting on a clean landing page.

Something between them survived every disagreement.

Mutual exhaustion with inefficiency.

They built their first prototype not for scale, but for relief—relief from friction unnoticed because it was universal.

Omar worked in concentrated bursts. Three hours of focus replaced entire days of traditional effort. When mental fatigue arrived, he stopped without guilt.

Kabir learned this rhythm slowly.

“At least pretend to struggle,” Kabir once joked, half-serious.

Omar didn’t look up from the screen. “Struggle doesn’t build things. It proves you were uncomfortable.”

Kabir laughed. “You’re going to offend an entire industry like this.”

"Good," Omar said. "They deserve better offenses."

***

The first failure arrived quietly.

They presented Nuclear Technologies' initial tool to a small institute owner who listened politely, nodded generously, and then declined without confrontation.

"Students won't understand something so simple," the man said. "They want dashboards. Complexity feels premium."

Kabir was visibly irritated after they left. "He didn't even try it."

"He didn't need to," Omar replied. "We failed to make the value obvious."

That night, Omar returned to the lodge alone and sat on the floor instead of the bed.

He replayed the pitch not emotionally but structurally.

Where had it relied on assumption instead of demonstration?

He dismantled the interface once more.

This time, he removed even more.

Money ran low.

Kabir took short freelance contracts to support shared expenses. Omar refused to do the same. Not out of pride—but because context switching scattered his clarity.

"You're still lazy," Kabir said one evening, counting cash. "Just differently."

Omar did not deny it.

"Yes," he said. "But I'm not careless."

They survived the weeks not on belief, but on patience. Each time doubt approached, reality countered it with small confirmations: faster execution, cleaner outcomes, interest shown by the right people instead of applause from the wrong ones.

The second presentation went better.

The third worked slowly.

The fourth transformed something small but measurable.

And then came the meeting that changed the trajectory without announcing itself as such.

A regional education network invited them to demonstrate Nuclear Technologies' system—not to buy, but to evaluate. Omar did not prepare extra slides. He prepared answers.

The room was filled with decision-makers who did not pretend to understand every technical detail.

"Why should we switch?" one of them asked.

"Because," Omar replied evenly, "your teams are busy maintaining activity instead of outcomes. This removes maintenance, not control."

"And if it fails?"

"Then you stop using it," Omar said. "Nothing locks you in."

That answer unsettled them.

When people are used to systems that demand loyalty, optionality feels radical.

They tested the prototype live.

Within minutes, one of the members leaned forward.

"This replaces three departments," she said quietly.

"It replaces friction," Omar corrected.

They approved a pilot.

Not a celebration. Not funding.

Just permission.

That was enough.

***

Nuclear Technologies began to exist outside conversation.

Users logged in. Data flowed. Support tickets dropped. Feedback focused on absence rather than presence—the absence of confusion, delay, repeated actions.

Omar monitored quietly.

Kabir celebrated loudly.

"You did this without grinding anyone," Kabir said one night, staring at usage metrics. "That's illegal somewhere, I think."

Omar watched the numbers climb steadily, not explosively.

“This is sustainable,” he said.

“That word scares investors,” Kabir replied.

“We’ll scare the right ones later.”

The nights blurred.

Sometimes Omar slept in the lodge. Sometimes on a borrowed mattress. Sometimes not at all—not from effort, but from attention fully engaged.

He noticed something else too.

The ease he felt was not joy.

It was alignment.

Effort rose only, when necessary, then dissolved. Solutions arrived not through force, but through removal. His nature—once criticized as lazy—had found terrain where speed mattered more than endurance.

One evening, after a long day refining onboarding flows, Omar closed his laptop and leaned back.

For the first time since leaving AnuNagari, he thought of home not as a place he had escaped—but as a baseline.

The quiet.
The routine.
The containment.

Nuclear Technologies carried that discipline at its core. Controlled output. Defined boundaries. High-impact minimalism.

Kabir broke the silence.

“This thing,” he said, nodding at the screen, “this is going to change how people build systems.”

Omar didn’t answer immediately.

He felt something deeper settle into place—a recognition not of success, but of inevitability.

“Yes,” he said at last. “If we don’t overwork it.”

For a few minutes they sat in that warm pool of electric light, watching numbers climb by small, steady increments. Kabir made a sound that was half-laugh, half-exhale.

“It’s less glamorous than I thought,” Kabir admitted. “But it’s also less fragile.”

Omar watched the dashboard as if it were a calming instrument. Each new user felt less like applause and more like calibration. He had expected louder reactions—fanfare, sudden invitations, superficial praise. Instead he got the subtler currency of adoption: a teacher logging in, a coordinator testing one workflow, a manager forwarding a link to a colleague.

That evening, after the lights in their makeshift office dimmed and the stall-owners began stacking the last of the chairs, Kabir pushed his chair back, stretched, and grinned.

“We should tell someone,” Kabir said, eyes bright.

“Not yet,” Omar replied. “We have to make sure it keeps behaving under small stress. One pilot doesn’t mean production.”

Kabir tried to argue the case for early exposure—investors, PR, visibility—but Omar held firm. He had seen how noise could consume the work itself, how applause shifted priorities from product to position. Nuclear Technologies had, so far, the rare advantage of being nimble and unnoticed. He intended to keep it that way until it ceased to be an advantage.

They left the building together, walking under a sky where the street-lamps pooled light rather than flood it. The city hummed with small dramas: a couple arguing over a borrowed fee, a chai vendor closing his shop with a practiced motion, a young man rehearsing a speech alone on a balcony.

Kabir kept talking—about possible features, about monetization models, about how to survive the inevitable failures. Omar listened and occasionally answered, but a quiet reconsideration had taken root in him: whatever scale they chased, it must preserve the central promise—less friction, not more features.

That night, Omar slept deeply.

Not because he was tired.

But because—for the first time—nothing inside him resisted tomorrow.

The next morning arrived without hesitation, sunlight slipping through the half-open window of the lodge, cutting a clean stripe across the floor. Omar woke with the strange clarity he had begun to recognize—an absence of internal noise. His mind wasn't racing toward outcomes or replaying failures; it was simply ready, as though sleep had performed a quiet audit of his thoughts overnight. He dressed without rush and stepped outside, feeling the city's morning rhythm align with him instead of overwhelm him.

Kabir joined him an hour later, hair messy, energy already buzzing at a higher frequency. "We need a demo video," he declared without greeting. "And a cleaner landing page. Something trustable. Something that doesn't look like two overworked founders in a rented room."

Omar smirked. "But that's exactly what we are."

"Yes," Kabir said, "which is why we need to look like we're not."

They walked toward a nearby chai stall, weaving through students carrying photocopies of forms they barely understood. Omar watched them—not with judgment, but with recognition. CoachingCity thrived on repetition. Students repeated attempts. Teachers repeated explanations. Systems repeated inefficiencies. Everyone worked hard, but often toward friction instead of away from it. Nuclear Technologies was the opposite: it thrived only when things became simpler.

As they sat down with their tea, Omar pulled out his notebook, flipping to a page filled with diagrams. Kabir leaned in, intrigued. "You're upgrading architecture?"

"No," Omar said. "I'm removing more."

Kabir groaned theatrically. "One day you will simplify so much, there will be nothing left except a blank screen."

“That blank screen,” Omar replied calmly, “might still solve more problems than half the software in this city.”

Kabir laughed, but the point wasn’t lost on him.

They spent the rest of the morning drafting user flows, not for complexity but for certainty. Each time Kabir suggested a flashy component—progress badges, gamified cues, animated panels—Omar crossed it out. “Users aren’t here to feel impressed,” he said. “They’re here to finish something quickly.”

By afternoon, Kabir no longer fought him. The design on the screen looked almost austere—a stark contrast to the crowded dashboards that dominated most educational platforms. But beneath that plainness lay something sharp and intentional. Purposeful absence. Necessary presence. A balance only Omar could articulate.

That evening, as they reviewed their progress, a faint breeze passed through the open window, lifting the corners of scattered papers. Kabir paused mid-sentence and looked at the interface again. “You know,” he said softly, “maybe the world doesn’t need more features. Maybe it just needs fewer excuses.”

Omar nodded once. “Exactly.”

They worked until night wrapped itself around the city again. And when they finally shut their laptops, neither felt drained. Only aligned.

Few days passed

*****

Chapter 5 – Things That Begin Quietly

There was nothing romantic about the morning.

The sky over CoachingCity was already bright, traffic moving with habitual impatience, horns filling the spaces where silence never survived. Omar arrived at the Nuclear Technologies office earlier than usual—not because he felt driven, but because mornings had become practical. Fewer interruptions. Cleaner thinking.

He parked his bike near the corner of the lot, removed his helmet, and checked his phone absently.

That was when he heard his name.

“Omar?”

He turned.

A woman stood a few steps away, holding a folder tightly against her chest. She looked uncertain—but not lost. Curious, but guarded. Her hair was tied back neatly, and the expression in her eyes suggested recognition struggling with disbelief.

“Yes?” he said.

She smiled, suddenly relieved. “It is you. I wasn’t sure.”

“I’m sorry—” Omar began, then stopped. Memory caught up. “Sana?”

She nodded, surprised he remembered without help. “Sana Khan. From college.”

Right.
A semester junior.
Quieter than most.
Sharp in group discussions, even sharper in silence.

“I didn’t expect to see you here,” she said. “I’m here for an interview.”

He gestured lightly toward the building. “Nuclear Technologies?”

“Yes.”

“So am I,” he replied.

Her eyebrows rose. “You work here?”

“Yes.”

That was true.

She smiled, relaxed just enough to step closer. “That’s... unexpected. I didn’t picture you in a place like this.”

Omar nodded. “Most people don’t.”

They shared a brief, awkward pause—the kind that occurs when two people realize the past has aged, but neither of them knows how much.

A security guard called out for her.

“That’s me,” she said quickly. “It was nice seeing you.”

“You too,” Omar replied.

She hesitated. "Maybe we'll talk after?"

"If you're free," he said.

She walked toward the entrance, then glanced back once. Omar watched her disappear inside before putting his helmet away.

He did not tell her anything.

Not because he planned deception—but because explanation would have disrupted something that had not yet decided what it was.

***

Sana's interview went longer than she expected.

The questions were precise without being hostile. The environment felt different from other offices she had visited—less performative, more intentional. No one tried to impress her with jargon. They asked how she approached problems. How she removed redundancy. How she handled ambiguity.

She answered honestly.

By the time she stepped out, her nervousness had dissolved into something closer to interest.

At the exit, she saw Omar again—standing near the coffee machine, scrolling through something on his phone.

"Still here?" she said lightly.

"I was busy," he replied.

They walked out together.

"What do you do here?" she asked.

"*Mostly solve problems before they become meetings*," he said.

She laughed. "That sounds useful."

"It is," he said. Then added, "Sometimes."

They ended up at a small café across the street, not by decision, but by default. They sat outside, ordered tea, and let conversation take shape naturally.

Sana spoke about interviews she had given; about how difficult it was to find places that didn't exhaust you before you started working. Omar listened carefully—not silently, but attentively. He asked questions that made her pause—not because they were difficult, but because they were rare.

"You don't sound impressed by titles," she observed at one point.

"I'm not," Omar replied. "Titles usually arrive after the interesting work is done."

She considered that. "Then what impresses you?"

He thought for a moment. "Clean thinking."

She smiled. "That explains why you didn't change much."

He looked at her. "Is that a compliment?"

"Yes," she said immediately. Then added, "I think."

***

Sana joined Nuclear Technologies the following week.

Not ceremoniously. Not dramatically.

She received an email, accepted it after a day, and showed up on Monday morning carrying mild excitement and cautious optimism. Omar made sure he was elsewhere when she arrived. Not avoidance—just distance.

He watched her from observation rather than intention.

She learned quickly. Asked better questions each day. She disliked unnecessary meetings and found pleasure in things working quietly. Omar noticed similarities immediately—and differences.

She worked steadily.

He worked selectively.

Somewhere in that difference, balance existed.

They spoke daily. Brief exchanges near desks. Longer conversations during breaks. Occasionally, laughter surfaced—unexpected and unplanned. Omar found himself waiting for those small moments without acknowledging it.

He did not complicate it.

He did not rush it.

Lazy, not careless.

***

On the fifth day, Sana frowned at her screen and muttered something under her breath.

Omar stopped by her desk. "Something wrong?"

She turned. "This doesn't make sense. The system is asking for three approvals where one would do."

Omar leaned in. “It shouldn’t.”

“It does.”

He scanned the workflow quickly. “You’re right.”

“Then why is it built like this?”

He removed her keyboard gently from her hands and made two changes.

“There,” he said. “It won’t ask anymore.”

She stared at the screen. “That’s it?”

“Yes.”

She leaned back slowly. “Why didn’t anyone else do that?”

“Because no one asked why it existed in the first place,” Omar replied.

She laughed—not loudly, but genuinely. “You’re dangerous.”

“That’s been said before,” he replied calmly.

Later that day, she caught him in the hallway.

“You’re not just a regular employee, are you?”

Omar met her gaze. “What makes you say that?”

“You speak like you can change things without permission.”

He smiled faintly. “Or maybe I just don’t enjoy asking.”

She studied him for a moment, then shook her head. “You’re strange.”

"Yes," he agreed.

And for the first time in a long while, the word felt accurate rather than dismissive.

***

The meeting invitation arrived on a Thursday afternoon.

Subject: Project Expansion – CEO Discussion
Attendees: Core Team + Strategy

Sana read it twice.

CEO.

She leaned back in her chair, nerves creeping in. She had assumed Nuclear Technologies was flatter—less hierarchical. But the word carried weight regardless.

She glanced across the office.

Omar wasn't at his desk.

When Friday arrived, the meeting began precisely on time. The room filled steadily. Sana sat near the middle, notebook open, posture composed.

The chair at the head of the table remained empty.

Ten minutes passed.

Then the door opened.

Omar walked in.

Not hurried. Not ceremonial.

He took the seat at the head of the table, placed his notebook down, and looked around the room.

"Let's start."

For a second, Sana did not breathe.

The sound in the room softened as reality rearranged itself inside her.

She looked again.

The posture.
The stillness.
The absence of performance.

It was him.

Her senior.
Her colleague.
The man who fixed workflows near coffee machines.

The CEO.

Omar's eyes met hers briefly—not apologetically, not proudly.

Just neutrally.

As if to say: *Nothing changed. You just saw it from a different angle.*

The presentation began.

And Sana listened—not just to the strategy, but to something else entirely.

The hum beneath clarity.

The meeting progressed, but Sana absorbed very little of its content in the beginning.

Her attention moved in fragments—his voice explaining timelines, his hands resting calmly on the table, the way others in the room deferred without hesitation. There was no exaggeration in him. No attempt to signal authority. The room obeyed him simply because it worked better when it did.

She realized something unsettled her more than the sudden revelation of his position.

Nothing about his behaviour had changed.

The same tone he used while speaking to engineers, he used with leaders. The same patience he showed at a desk-side discussion, he applied to strategy. There was no performance switch, no elevation of self.

That consistency disturbed her expectations.

When the meeting ended, chairs shifted, conversations resumed in low voices. People gathered their things quickly, some eager to follow up, others relieved it was over. Sana remained seated for a moment longer than necessary.

Omar stood, closed his notebook, and addressed the room with a final sentence that felt more concluding than formal. Then he turned to leave.

This time, he stopped near her.

“You handled the workflow issue well,” he said quietly. “Good catch.”

She looked up at him, searching his face for signs of deliberate concealment. There were none.

“You could have told me,” She said.

“Yes,” he replied. “But it wouldn’t have helped either of us.”

That answer lingered heavier than she expected.

He nodded once, then walked away, already absorbed back into motion, into responsibility, into a role that now extended far beyond the casual familiarity she had begun forming.

Sana remained seated, aware of something new settling into place.

Not disappointment.

Curiosity—with weight.

***

Sana did not speak to Omar for the rest of the day.

Not deliberately. Not pointedly. The opportunities simply did not arise in a way that would have felt natural. Meetings pulled people into smaller rooms. Desks became islands again. Routine resumed as if nothing fundamental had shifted.

But something had.

She replayed moments she hadn't paid attention to earlier—the ease with which he moved through the office, the way people deferred without seeking reassurance, the absence of urgency in his presence. She had mistaken familiarity for equality, structure for coincidence.

The realization unsettled her, not because he was the CEO, but because he had chosen not to be perceived as one.

That choice mattered.

Over the next few days, Sana watched Omar more carefully.

Not with suspicion. With recalibration.

He did not begin asserting authority where he hadn't before. He didn't correct her tone, didn't create distance, didn't suddenly become formal. If anything, he became more restrained—speaking less, listening more, offering clarity only when it removed confusion rather than asserted position.

She noticed how he stepped back when discussions grew crowded, how he allowed others to arrive at conclusions he had already formed, intervening only when momentum risked becoming noise.

This restraint intrigued her.

Ambition she understood.
Competence she respected.

But this—this quiet refusal to dominate—required more effort than command.

One afternoon, she confronted the question silently.

Would I have spoken to him the same way if I had known?

The answer formed without resistance.

Yes.

And that answer surprised her.

***

The work itself deepened their interaction.

They began collaborating on a project that lived in the inconvenient space between technical clarity and human behaviour. Sana approached it analytically, structuring solutions through incremental testing. Omar approached it subtractively, removing assumptions without apology.

Their differences sharpened the work.

One evening, they stayed late—not because deadlines loomed, but because the system had reached a point where leaving felt disruptive. The office thinned slowly, then emptied, lights switching off row by row.

Sana leaned back in her chair. “You knew this would work.”

Omar shook his head. “I knew what would fail.”

“That’s not the same.”

“But it’s more reliable.”

She smiled faintly. “You’re difficult.”

“Yes,” he said. “Consistently.”

Silence followed—not awkward, not charged. Just present.

It occurred to Sana then that silence around him felt different. It did not demand filling. It did not rush toward resolution. It waited.

She realized she felt rested in it.

***

The question she avoided finally surfaced when she least expected it.

They were walking out together, late evening air cutting through the city's leftover heat. She stopped near the gate.

"Did you ever plan to tell me?" she asked.

Omar considered the question carefully. "About what?"

She held his gaze. "About who you are here."

"I told you what I do," he said. "That remains accurate."

"That's not an answer."

"No," he admitted. "It's a boundary."

She accepted that more easily than she thought she would. "Why?"

"Because roles interfere with observation," he said. "I wanted to know how you think when no rank exists between us."

"That sounds calculated."

"Yes."

"And dishonest."

"No," he said gently. "Incomplete."

She studied him—not defensively, but intently. "And now that I know?"

He shrugged. "Now we adjust. Or we don't."

That unsettled her.

He was not negotiating outcomes.
He was offering reality.

***

Adjustment came slowly.

There were days Sana found herself stepping back, instinctively editing her words before speaking to him, then annoyed with herself for doing so. There were moments when she caught others watching her interactions with Omar more closely, reevaluating proximity in the light of hierarchy.

None of it came from him.

That, more than anything, anchored her.

They stopped meeting at the café across the street, replaced by longer walks after work, conversations that unfolded without agenda. Topics shifted away from projects into quieter territories—education as industry, childhood memory, the exhaustion of constant evaluation.

Omar spoke little of himself, but when he did, the details were precise rather than embellished. He did not dramatize struggle. He did not frame success as inevitability. He described circumstances the way others described weather.

It made his accomplishments feel less impressive and more unsettling.

One evening, Sana asked, “Do you care what people think of you here?”

Omar responded without thought. “No.”

She believed him instantly.

“Most people say that,” she said. “Few mean it.”

He looked at her. "Most people build themselves by trying to fit expectations. I remove expectations that don't serve something real."

"Does that get lonely?"

"Yes," he said. Then added, "But it's quiet."

***

The attraction arrived unnoticed.

Not as urgency. Not as desire demanding articulation.

It presented itself instead as preference.

Sana noticed she waited for his input even when she didn't need approval. Omar noticed he adjusted priorities more readily when she was involved. They found themselves arguing less and refining more, disagreement evolving into precision.

Neither named it.

They were both practiced at disassembly. Naming things created shape, and shape invited interference.

Late one night, while reviewing feedback, Sana laughed unexpectedly.

"What?" Omar asked.

"I just realized something," she said.

"That's rarely harmless."

She met his eyes. "You're the first person I've worked with who never tries to impress me."

He held her gaze evenly. "You don't require it."

That sentence stayed with her long after they left the office.

***

There was a moment—small, unremarkable to anyone else—when Sana understood something irreversible had happened.

They were sharing a ride partway home, city lights blurring past. A sudden stop sent her lurching forward slightly. Omar reacted instinctively, steadying her with a hand at her elbow.

The contact lasted no more than a second.

He pulled away immediately, expression unchanged.

But the space between them did not reset.

Sana felt it distinctly—the shift from abstraction to awareness.

She did not look at him. Neither did he speak.

The car resumed motion.

Nothing dramatic followed. No apology. No acknowledgment.

That restraint carried more weight than confession ever could.

Weeks passed.

The company grew quieter, stronger. Nuclear Technologies accumulated trust through absence—absence of friction, confusion, delay. Omar remained firm in one thing: growth would follow clarity, not precede it.

Sana began receiving attention of a different kind—invited into discussions earlier, consulted without prompt, her judgments trusted. Some of that traced back to proximity. Most of it earned itself.

Her family noticed changes before she named them internally.

“You sound steadier,” her mother commented during a call.

Sana smiled. “I am.”

She did not mention Omar.

Not yet.

***

One evening, after a long stretch of work and near silence, Sana stopped walking abruptly.

“You know this is happening,” she said.

Omar looked at her. “Yes.”

“That it complicates things.”

“Yes.”

“That it might cost something.”

He nodded. “Everything costs.”

She exhaled slowly. “Why are you not stopping it?”

He answered without hesitation. “Because nothing about this feel forced.”

There was no confession in his voice.

Only acknowledgment.

She took a step closer. Not touching. Not retreating.

“Then we proceed carefully,” she said.

“Yes,” Omar agreed.

That was the closest they came to a promise.

In the weeks that followed, their closeness did not expand outward.

It deepened inward.

They did not inform anyone. They did not change behaviour. They simply aligned—work flowing more precisely, silences growing more comfortable, understanding arriving earlier.

The absence of declaration did not diminish its reality.

If anything, it protected it.

Omar knew something else, though he did not say it aloud.

This—this quiet alignment—was fragile not because of emotion, but because of the world it would eventually have to meet.

Success reshapes perception.
Visibility invites judgment.

And Sana’s world—beyond office walls—was not built to accept alignment without credentials.

She knew this. Omar knew this. Yet neither of them tried to dissect that future. What existed between them lived in the quiet hours before deadlines and after clarity, in the small spaces where conversation softened instead of intensifying.

What surprised Sana most was how ordinary Omar was in those moments.

Not simple.
Not dull.
Just... ordinary in the way rare people sometimes are—comfortable with silence, comfortable with being misunderstood, comfortable with letting others talk themselves into exhaustion while he waited for the essential point to surface.

That steadiness made him disarming.

It also made him difficult to categorize.

One afternoon, while they were reviewing user flows, Sana caught herself studying him again—not his expression, but the way he moved. There was no wasted energy in him. He did not fidget. He did not gesture broadly. He did not decorate his intent with performance.

He simply existed with purpose.

“What?” he asked without looking up.

“Nothing,” she said quickly.

“Then stop staring,” he replied calmly.

She flushed. “I wasn’t—”

“You were.”

She looked away, flustered but amused at his lack of theatrics. Most men would have teased. Most would have turned it into flirtation. Omar named the reality and returned to the task.

His refusal to dramatize things gave every interaction weight.

***

Kabir noticed nothing—or pretended not to.

He continued bouncing between deadlines and excitement, storming into the office with new ideas every morning, declaring breakthroughs that rarely survived the afternoon. He often called Sana for quick suggestions, and she often intercepted his chaotic enthusiasm with structured notes.

“Thank God you joined,” Kabir told her one evening, sprawled across a chair. “Omar would have fired me by now if you weren’t balancing the equations.”

Sana smiled. “I don’t think he would fire you.”

Kabir snorted. “He won’t. That’s the problem. He’ll just reduce my responsibilities until I fade from the system.”

She glanced at Omar, who was working quietly nearby. “He doesn’t do anything accidentally.”

“Exactly!” Kabir whispered, eyes widening dramatically. “He’s too intentional. It scares me.”

Sana nearly answered *It steadies me,* but she said nothing.

She and Omar often found themselves staying back after others had left—not intentionally, but because their work rhythms matched. He would refine logic while she structured communication, each adjusting slightly based on the other’s presence.

One such evening, she closed her laptop and found Omar standing by the window, looking at the street where dim lamps cast amber halos on the pavement.

"Does this ever overwhelm you?" she asked, approaching him.

"What?"

"The responsibility. Being the one people look to."

"No," he said. "Responsibility becomes overwhelming only when you pretend to be something you're not."

"And you don't?"

He glanced at her. "I don't have the patience to perform."

She smiled at that. "I think that's your superpower."

"It's laziness," he corrected.

"It's discipline."

"No," he said. "Discipline is consistency despite discomfort. I remove the discomfort."

She laughed softly. "That's such an Omar sentence."

"And what does that mean?"

"That you simplify yourself the way you simplify systems."

He didn't argue.

There were days when Sana felt the weight of the secret between them—not the emotional connection, but the unspoken acknowledgment that he was not just a colleague. The dual identities sat strangely in her mind: Omar the teammate, Omar the founder, Omar the man who answered softly when she asked hard questions.

But he never used his position to alter the balance between them. If anything, he used it to protect it.

Sometimes, when they walked together after work, she sensed him adjusting his pace—not slowing down for her, not speeding up, but matching the rhythm without making it visible. That subtlety made her more aware than any explicit gesture could have.

"You think too loudly," he said once during such a walk.

Sana blinked. "What does that even mean?"

"You think in visible patterns," he said. "It shows on your face."

"And you?"

"My thoughts don't like the spotlight."

She nudged him lightly with her elbow. "You're insufferable."

"Yes," he replied. "But predictably."

***

At work, she began learning his signatures—how he fell silent right before he removed an unnecessary feature, how he tapped his pen twice before making a decision, how he gave answers in the form of constraints instead of declarations.

"You don't think in possibilities," she observed one day.

"No."

"You think in exclusions."

"Yes."

"And that doesn't limit you?"

"It frees me," he said simply. "A problem becomes solvable once you know what it isn't."

She found herself absorbing that approach unconsciously. Her work sharpened, her questions became more precise, and her sense of direction grew steadier. She understood then that being near him didn't make her dependent—it made her disciplined.

Omar was felted

For now, though, the dream allowed it.

And Omar, living inside its impossible generosity, let the moment exist without demanding its future.

*****

Chapter 6 – Becoming Acceptable

Success did not arrive like a celebration. It arrived like a correction.

There was no announcement within Nuclear Technologies when the first major contract finalized. No applause. No speeches. The agreement appeared quietly in shared documents, signed and filed with the same restraint that governed everything else Omar allowed to grow.

Still, things changed.

People outside the company began saying the name more often—sometimes incorrectly, sometimes with emphasis, sometimes with curiosity that had not existed before. Nuclear Technologies moved from being a quiet solution to a referenced one. Meetings that once required explanation now required presence.

Omar remained unchanged.

Or so it appeared.

Internally, he noticed shifts immediately. Requests came earlier. Decisions carried longer consequences. The margin for silence narrowed. None of this bothered him. It merely demanded a different calibration.

Sana sensed it before it affected her directly.

She saw the way Omar absorbed pressure without absorbing tension—how he deflected urgency, reframed panic into structure, and refused to let speed masquerade as progress. He never appeared rushed; instead, the world around him adjusted its pace reluctantly, then inevitably.

And people noticed.

***

The first comment from the outside came indirectly.

Sana was visiting her family one weekend, sitting in the living room while her mother folded freshly washed clothes. The television hummed softly in the background—news scrolling beneath a discussion panel focused on emerging technology firms.

Her mother glanced at the screen.

"They're talking about some new company again," she said casually. "Nuclear something."

Sana looked up.

The segment was brief, unsensational. A passing reference to operational efficiency within educational ecosystems. No faces shown. Just a name.

"Nuclear Technologies," Sana said.

Her mother nodded. "Yes. That."

The moment passed. But something registered quietly in Sana's chest—not pride, not alarm. Recognition.

She said nothing further.

She was not ready to speak yet.

...

...

Resistance did not emerge dramatically.

It surfaced in subtler forms.

Her family began asking questions that had structure but no stated intent. About where she worked. About how stable it was. About who ran it. About where it might lead.

Sana answered honestly without elaborating.

“There’s growth,” she said when asked.

“How much?” her uncle pressed once.

“Enough,” she replied.

She noticed the questions grew more frequent when relatives visited, more pointed when acquaintances joined conversations. Approval, she realized, followed structure—not understanding.

And Omar, by nature, disrupted structure.

***

At work, proximity became more visible.

Not because of behaviour—but because of patterns.

Sana was consistently looped into discussions early. Her judgment carried weight. Omar did not protect her from scrutiny, nor did he elevate her unnaturally. He trusted her capacity and allowed it to reveal itself.

This earned respect internally.

Externally, it provoked assumptions.

People began noticing.

“Are you... close to him?” someone asked her once, carefully.

Sana answered evenly. “We work well together.”

That was enough to stop conversation, but not speculation.

She knew what that meant.

Alignment becomes visible long before intention is spoken.

The question that frightened her most arrived at dinner.

“What kind of family does your CEO come from?” her mother asked one evening, eyes still on the plate she was serving.

The tone wasn’t accusatory.

It was evaluative.

Sana hesitated. “Middle-class,” she said. “Quiet background.”

“And education?”

“Technical. University-level.”

Her mother nodded slowly. “Religion?”

Sana met her gaze. “Muslim.”

That answer changed the temperature of the room—slightly, but distinctly.

“And caste?” her aunt asked.

Sana stiffened. “That’s not how—”

"I know," the woman cut in gently. "But families still ask."

Sana did not answer immediately. The silence elongated without becoming confrontational.

"I don't know," she said finally.

The omission was not accidental.

Her family absorbed it without comment.

That worried her more than disagreement would have.

***

Omar learned of this resistance indirectly.

He noticed it in Sana's posture more than her words.

She became careful in ways she hadn't been. Slightly guarded when speaking about home. Thoughtful where she had previously been fluid.

One evening, while standing outside the office as traffic slowed, he addressed it directly.

"They won't accept me," she said, before he could ask.

It wasn't fear in her voice.

It was clarity.

Omar nodded. "Not yet."

She looked at him sharply. "You're not offended?"

"No," he said. "They're reacting to uncertainty. That's rational."

"To them," she said.

"And to statistics," he replied calmly.

That response unsettled her.

"You're not a statistic," she said.

"I am," he replied. "Until proven otherwise."

She folded her arms. "And how do you plan to be proven?"

"I don't," he said. "Time does."

She studied him. "You're very calm about being rejected."

"I'm not being rejected," he said evenly. "I'm being evaluated."

"That's worse."

"Yes," he agreed. "But less personal."

They stood quietly after that.

Sana realized then that Omar had lived under evaluation for most of his life—by institutions, by opportunity, by absence. This was merely another framework attempting to measure him by external markers.

Markers he had not prioritized.

***

Public recognition arrived shortly thereafter.

An article featured Nuclear Technologies in a long-form analysis of scalable systems. Omar's name appeared once—without photograph, without biography.

Still, it circulated.

Her cousin mentioned it casually during a phone call. "Isn't that where you work?"

"Yes," Sana replied.

"And the CEO—has an unusual style," the cousin added, half-admiring, half-curious.

"How so?"

"He avoids spotlight. That usually means confidence."

That observation travelled quickly.

Confidence, Sana knew, was an acceptable trait.

Even when origins were questioned.

At the next family gathering, the tone shifted.

Questions remained, but they reorganized.

"So this company is growing?"
"Yes."
"Clients outside the state?"
"Yes."
"Long-term prospects?"
"Yes."

Sana answered without embellishment.

Her mother listened carefully, nodding more often than she interrupted.

“What does he want?” her mother asked afterward, alone.

Sana did not pretend not to understand the question.

“He wants to build well,” she said. “He doesn’t rush.”

Her mother exhaled softly. “Men like that either succeed or wound quietly.”

Sana met her gaze. “He doesn’t wound.”

Her mother didn’t reply immediately.

“I don’t doubt his character,” she said finally. “I doubt whether the world will allow it.”

Sana had no answer for that.

***

At work, momentum increased.

Nuclear Technologies expanded selectively, refusing deals that required compromise of structure. This frustrated some potential partners and impressed others. Omar remained consistent: growth would not outpace comprehension.

Sana admired this about him.

She also feared it.

Because acceptance—for families like hers—often followed visibility, not restraint.

One night, as they reviewed long-term projections, Sana spoke carefully.

“If success becomes visible enough,” she said, “people stop asking where you come from.”

Omar looked at the data on-screen. “They start asking why you think you deserve it.”

She sighed. “That doesn’t scare you?”

“No,” he replied. “That question assumes competition. I don’t compete that way.”

She studied him. “You’re certain this will work.”

He shook his head. “No. I’m certain I won’t change how I work to make it work.”

That answer frightened her slightly.

It also grounded her.

The first formal resistance arrived in silence.

An invitation that never came.
A response delayed beyond politeness.
A conversation redirected.

Sana recognized these patterns easily.

She did not bring them up immediately.

Not because she was avoiding the truth—but because she wanted to see whether Omar noticed them too. He did.

He simply chose not to name them yet.

Becoming acceptable, Omar understood, was not about proving worth.

It was about exhausting alternatives to acceptance.

And that process had already begun.

***

The confrontation did not happen in one explosive moment.

It arrived in stages, measured and methodical, the way decisions rooted in tradition often did. Sana sensed it first when discussions about her future began including pauses—deliberate, weighted silences meant to invite correction.

Her family did not object outright. They asked, instead, for clarity.

"Where is this heading?" her mother asked one evening, voice calm, eyes steady.

Sana did not soften the answer. "Forward."

"Toward what?" her uncle pressed. "Marriage? Or just work?"

The discomfort was familiar. So was the implication: time was being measured not in years but in social viability.

"I don't separate them," Sana said. "The person is the direction."

Silence followed, heavier than argument.

When Omar came up directly, it was not framed as objection.

"He seems capable," her uncle admitted during a later conversation. "But capability alone is not a foundation."

"For what?" Sana asked quietly.

"For permanence," her aunt replied.

Sana felt irritation rise but tempered it. "Permanence is built, not inherited."

"That's a modern interpretation," her uncle replied. "Families look at background because they cannot evaluate uncertainty."

Sana wanted to argue. Instead, she listened.

They were not asking whether Omar was good.

They were asking whether he was safe.

***

That distinction reached Omar eventually, not through Sana's words but through what she left unsaid.

He sensed the recalibration in her tone—the way she spoke with composure instead of enthusiasm, precision instead of warmth. One evening, after a long workday, he addressed it directly.

"They've escalated," he said calmly.

"Yes," Sana replied. "They want assurance."

He nodded slowly. "And you?"

She hesitated. "I want them to stop treating you like a probability."

Omar smiled faintly. "Then they'll need data."

She looked at him sharply. "Is that how you see this?"

"Yes," he said. "Their resistance isn't emotional. It's statistical."

That unnerved her.

"So you plan to out-perform the doubt?" she asked.

"I plan to persist," Omar replied evenly. "Performance follows."

She studied him. "And if it doesn't?"

"Then I accept the result without resentment."

That frightened her more than optimism would have.

***

Time intervened, as Omar had predicted.

Nuclear Technologies crossed a threshold quietly—a partnership with a national entity that brought visibility without requiring spectacle. The agreement was referenced in industry circles first, then in mainstream discourse. Meetings multiplied. Consultants began asking questions differently.

Omar's world widened without his consent. And Sana's family noticed.

"It seems your company is doing well," her mother remarked one evening, the observation wrapped carefully in understatement.

"Yes," Sana replied.

"How involved is he—personally?" her aunt asked.

"He built it," Sana said. "And he runs it."

Those changed things.

From that point onward, conversations shifted tone. Where there had once been concern, there was now curiosity. Where there had been hesitation, calculation replaced it.

Omar was no longer a question mark.

He was a variable trending upward.

The visit was polite.

Civil.

Measured.

Omar arrived dressed simply. He spoke sparingly, answering questions directly without embellishment. He did not justify his choices or frame his background as triumph. He explained his work in terms of process rather than profit.

That unsettled some of them.

Others leaned forward.

“What about stability?” her uncle asked.

“I design for it,” Omar replied. “That doesn’t guarantee it. But it increases probability.”

Her mother observed him without speaking much, eyes sharper than her posture suggested.

Later, alone in the kitchen, she asked Sana a single question.

“Does he adjust for you?”

Sana answered without thought. “Yes. But he doesn’t disappear.”

Her mother nodded, something unreadable passing through her expression.

***

Acceptance did not arrive as approval.

It arrived as permission.

Permission to continue seeing each other without objection. Permission to include Omar's name in discussions without tension. Permission to imagine futures without immediate cancellation.

This was not celebration.

It was compliance.

Sana realized the cost immediately.

Love, filtered through acceptability, lost some of its innocence.

Omar sensed it too.

One evening, after leaving her house, he walked beside her quietly.

"They didn't accept me," he said. "They accepted my trajectory."

She stopped walking. "Is that enough for you?"

"For now," he replied honestly.

"For me, too," she admitted. "But it shouldn't have to be."

"No," Omar agreed. "But that's not the world we're in."

She took his hand briefly, then let go.

Distance, she realized, was now strategic.

Later that night, Sana sat beside Omar, both of them quiet.

"They accept you," she said eventually.

Omar looked ahead, considering. “They accept what I represent.”

She sighed. “That distinction matters to you.”

“Yes,” he said. “It will matter more with time.”

“You’re thinking ahead again.”

“I always do,” he replied. “It’s safer there.”

She smiled faintly. “For someone who doesn’t rush, you think very far.”

He looked at her then. “Because rushing and thinking are not the same.”

Becoming acceptable came at a cost neither of them voiced.

For Sana, it meant watching her love translated into credentials.

For Omar, it meant understanding that success had become his introduction before his character.

Neither resented it.

But neither celebrated it either.

They moved forward anyway—aware that acceptance, once earned this way, could always be revoked the same way.

And somewhere beneath that awareness, deeper questions began forming.

Questions about time.
About permanence.
About whether success, like dreams, demanded eventual payment.

For now, the dream remained generous.

And Omar, living inside its widening corridors, continued forward—methodical, composed, and increasingly difficult to measure by ordinary means.

That night, after Sana returned to her room, Omar stood alone on the balcony, city lights stretching outward in disciplined rows. From this height, everything looked organized—paths visible, distances measured, destinations implied. It reminded him of systems he designed: comprehensible from above, complicated only up close.

He understood now that acceptance was never absolute. It moved with circumstances, adjusted with performance, tightened when uncertainty returned. People did not anchor trust in character; they anchored it in continuity.

That realization did not make him bitter.

It made him precise.

Inside the room, Sana sat quietly, phone untouched in her hands, feeling the subtle shift from resistance to regulation. The world had not changed its rules for them—it had merely allowed an exception, conditional and revisable.

Neither of them said it aloud, but both felt it:

What required continual proof was not permanence. It was momentum.

And momentum, once achieved, rarely allowed rest.

As they prepared for sleep that night, the future no longer appeared as a decision waiting to be made, but as time beginning to accelerate—folding itself forward, years compressing toward outcomes neither of them could yet see, but both had already stepped into.

***

They lived the next days under a new light that was both practical and strangely fragile. Invitations arrived with measured courtesy—breakfasts at acquaintances' homes, a polite request to speak at a small seminar, a congratulatory text from an old professor. Each item on the calendar felt like permission issued in small stamps rather than a wholehearted welcome. Omar attended some, declined others; his refusals were as calm as his acceptances, and both read as intentional rather than defensive.

Sana watched how people began to look at him differently: with an evaluating patience that had once belonged only to employers and investors. Her colleagues asked his opinion in passing, then repeated it in meetings as if hearing it twice made it more authoritative. Friends who owed him nothing now called to ask about collaborations. Her family, relieved by the shifting tone of conversations, relaxed in subtle ways—a loose question became less probing, a pause shortened. Yet in private, her mother still asked about background the way one checks a recipe's ingredients: discreet, habitual, and impossible to ignore.

Omar felt the change as a narrowing of margin. Where before there had been room for error, now outcomes mattered more than intent. He did not resent it; he recognized it as consequence. He woke earlier, not because of ambition but because calibration required time. He began to log small metrics—uptime, daily active users, support tickets closed—less as obsession and more as a quiet ledger of fidelity. Numbers, he had discovered, were persuasive when words were not.

They preserved a private economy between themselves: small rituals that resisted publicity. A shared round of tea after late nights. A message that read only "Safe?" when either of them travelled. Tiny, private confirmations that the public narrative could not touch. These gestures mattered because they were unremarked upon; they remained a space neither checks nor reports.

At times, the pressure was a distant hum; at other times it felt intimate, as if the world had drawn a circle close enough that missteps echoed. Both of them adjusted—Sana by learning the vocabulary of probability and presentation, Omar by refusing the allure of spectacle. Together they practiced that odd discipline: building something useful in the plain light of everyday work, while keeping their shared life small enough to hold.

*****

Chapter 7 – When Years Start Folding

Time did not accelerate all at once.

It bent.

Omar noticed it first in small, dismissible ways—things most people would attribute to routine or growing responsibility. Meetings that felt resolved before they began. Projects concluding without the emotional residue of closure. Achievements announced that felt like confirmations of something already completed.

At first, this felt like mastery.

Then it began to feel like subtraction.

Nuclear Technologies entered what journalists later referred to as its "silent expansion phase." The term amused Omar when he first read it because nothing about the growth felt noisy from the inside. Offices opened not as events but as necessities. Teams formed as problems demanded solutions. Systems evolved without drama.

The company no longer reacted to opportunity.

Opportunity adapted to it.

Omar's role shifted accordingly. He stopped answering operational questions altogether and focused on structural ones—decisions that would not show results for years, but would determine whether those years felt stable or chaotic. He spoke less in meetings, but when he did, the room became still.

This did not flatter him.

It concerned him.

He remembered when his presence had required explanation.

Now it required calibration.

The marriage happened in the same way everything else did—cleanly.

No spectacle. No prolonged negotiation. Sana's family framed it as resolution rather than celebration, which suited Omar. The ceremony was modest, efficient, dignified. Guests complimented the orderliness of it, mistaking absence of chaos for serenity.

Sana noticed this immediately.

The morning after the wedding, she stood at the window of their apartment, watching the city arrange itself below. Omar stood beside her, quiet, present, holding a cup of tea he had already forgotten to drink.

"That was fast," she said.

"Yes," he replied.

She turned to face him. "Not the ceremony. Us."

Omar considered the word.

"Continuation usually is," he said. "Beginnings feel slower."

She smiled, uncertain whether that reassured her or unsettled her.

Marriage changed nothing fundamental between them.

That was both its strength and its fracture point.

***

The first sign that years were folding appeared during a family visit.

Omar noticed his father's hands before anything else—how they shook slightly when lifting a glass, how the grip had weakened without comment. His mother repeated a question she had already asked earlier in the day, then laughed it off before he could respond.

Later that night, Omar lay awake, watching the ceiling fan.

Last visit, his father had been fine.

Last visit had been... when?

The time between those visits tugged uncomfortably at his memory. It existed, but only as structure—calendar entries, travel bookings, task resumptions. The feeling of those months had dissolved.

He understood then that memory was no longer mapping experience accurately.

It was archiving outcome.

The children arrived without drama too.

The first one changed something immediately—and then, paradoxically, not at all. Omar held the child with care, attentive and precise, aware of responsibility arriving with irreversible weight. Love followed, but it felt... familiar.

Not predicted.

Recognized.

The second child reinforced the pattern.

Moments and milestones began stacking rather than unfolding. Omar did not feel absent emotionally; he felt pre-complete, as though each experience arrived already integrated into something larger.

This frightened him, though he did not say so.

Sana noticed.

"You're here," she said one night, watching him watch their children sleep. "But you're already ahead."

He did not deny it. "I think I'm losing sync."

"With what?"

"With sequence," he replied. "Things arrive out of order emotionally."

She frowned slightly. "That sounds like exhaustion."

"No," Omar said. "Exhaustion fades. This clarifies."

She said nothing after that.

She knew when to let questions wait.

Friends began to fade without argument.

Majid called once every few months now, always apologetic in tone despite neither of them demanding frequency. His life had organized itself into manageable simplicity—work, family, adjusted ambition. He sounded content.

Hazir called less often but spoke more deeply when he did.

One evening, after a long silence, Hazir asked him directly, "Do you feel like you're still arriving somewhere?"

Omar looked out over the city before answering. "No. I feel like I'm managing transit."

"That doesn't sound peaceful."

"It's efficient," Omar replied.

Hazir paused. "Efficiency isn't comfort."

"No," Omar agreed. "But it sustains motion."

Hazir sighed softly. "Just don't forget motion isn't the same as meaning."

Omar did not respond.

He was busy noticing that the advice sounded like something he had already heard.

Or already given.

Or not needed anymore.

***

Years compressed further.

Children grew into routines Omar observed rather than experienced. Sana aged gracefully, growing into herself with a steadiness that sometimes unsettled him. She remained present in moments he analysed later rather than occupied fully while they happened.

She accused him of nothing.

That hurt more than accusation would have.

One afternoon, while reviewing strategy documents, Omar paused mid-sentence. The room had gone quiet. His team waited.

“I think we’ve already solved this,” he said.

They exchanged glances.

“How?” someone asked.

Omar opened his mouth, then stopped.

“I don’t remember,” he admitted. “But I’m certain.”

They trusted him.

That frightened him more than doubt ever had.

The body noticed what the mind dismissed.

Sleep began arriving unevenly. Dreams extended into waking moments. Omar occasionally felt the residue of conversations before they happened—not thoughts, but impressions.

Once, he answered a question Sana hadn’t yet asked.

She stared at him. “I haven’t said anything.”

He nodded slowly. “I know.”

The quiet between them lengthened—not with suspicion, but concern.

This life was... correct.

Too correct.

Omar felt as if he were watching a model run at accelerated speed, each cycle functioning exactly as designed.

He had built systems like this before.

They always broke.

The chapter of becoming acceptable had closed quietly.

Now another had opened—one without name or permission.

One afternoon, while standing by the window, looking over a city that no longer surprised him, Omar felt it distinctly:

Time was no longer moving *with* him.

It was moving *through* him.

And he was not certain how many years it had left to spend.

***

The first school bag arrived on a quiet morning.

It stood upright near the door, bright against the neutral tones of the apartment, unused and expectant. Omar stopped as he passed it, one hand still resting on his phone, as though the bag had appeared without warning.

"When did that happen?" he asked.

Sana looked up from the kitchen. "Yesterday. You were on a call."

He nodded once. The answer fit too easily.

The child—no, his child—ran toward him, shoes half-worn, voice sharp with excitement. Omar crouched instinctively, adjusting straps, tying laces that had already been tied once before. The motions came from memory deeper than recall.

"You're late," Sana said lightly.

"I know," Omar replied. He always did.

That morning, as he watched them leave, Omar stood longer than necessary at the door. He tried to fix the sequence in his mind: child at home, child in school, years passing between those states. But the sensation of time refused to stretch.

It folded instead—cleanly, efficiently.

Work slowed deliberately.

Not because demand decreased, but because Omar insisted on depth over expansion. Nuclear Technologies declined three acquisition offers and walked away from a government project that required compromise. Advisors pushed back politely, then more firmly.

"Speed matters now," one of them said across a long table.

"Speed has always mattered," Omar replied. "It just matters least when everyone is chasing it."

Some nodded. Others grew quiet.

He did not misinterpret the silence.

Trust was thinning.

The kind of success he practiced did not scale emotionally. It demanded patience from people rewarded by motion.

He accepted that.

Home became the place where time most clearly broke its rules.

Children grew between meals. Language appeared where silence had been. Interests formed and hardened as though their growth operated on a schedule separate from his awareness.

One evening, Sana corrected their younger child gently, then met Omar's eyes.

"You missed that sentence," she said calmly.

"I was here," he replied.

"I know. But you weren't with it."

That distinction hurt.

He tried to be more present after that. Tried listening without planning responses. Tried staying with moments until they concluded naturally.

It helped.

Briefly.

Then the sensation returned—that he was entering scenes too late or leaving them too early, never precisely aligned with the center of them.

***

Majid visited once, unexpectedly.

He had gained weight and lost hurry. His laughter came slower but stayed longer. He sat comfortably in the unfamiliar living room, looking around with open curiosity.

"You did well," Majid said, not with envy but acknowledgment.

Omar poured tea. "So did you."

Majid shook his head. "I adjusted."

They shared a look full of old context.

"For what it's worth," Majid added, "this life suits you more than the waiting one."

Omar nodded. "It suits my system."

Majid smiled. "Not everything is a system."

After he left, Omar replayed that line.

It lodged itself somewhere unwelcome.

Hazir's visit followed months later.

Hazir observed more than he spoke. He noticed the bookshelf first, then the thresholds between rooms, then the view from the window.

"You built this like a transition space," Hazir said finally.

"How so?"

"Everything leads somewhere else. Very little asks you to stay."

Omar considered the apartment differently after that.

"I don't resist staying," he said.

"No," Hazir agreed. "You just don't depend on it."

That was not meant as criticism.

It still unsettled him.

***

One night, long after everyone was asleep, Omar sat at the dining table alone. Papers lay scattered in front of him—budget projections, timelines, expansions planned years ahead.

He noticed something odd.

The handwriting on older notes matched newer ones exactly.

No change in pressure. No adjustment in rhythm. The writing of a man who had not aged internally.

His body felt older.

His responsibilities had multiplied.

But the self-doing the work had not shifted.

He closed the papers and rested his forehead against his hands.

"What are you missing?" he asked softly, not expecting an answer.

The silence did not respond.

The body, however, continued its own commentary.

Sometimes when he stood, dizziness followed briefly. Once, while playing with the children, his vision narrowed for a second too long. Sana noticed immediately.

“You need rest,” she said.

“I rest,” he replied.

She shook her head. “You reset. That’s different.”

He did not argue.

That night, he dreamed of a train station—not any in particular, but familiar in structure. Trains arrived and left without announcement. He stood on the platform unsure whether he was early or late.

When he woke up, the intent of the dream remained, even as the details dissolved.

He began writing it down.

***

Despite everything, there were moments of undeniable warmth.

A shared laugh mid-argument. The children’s stories before sleep. Sana’s hand resting on his shoulder while he worked silently beside her.

These moments felt real.

Almost anchoring.

He began looking for them consciously, documenting them inwardly, measuring their solidity.

It was work.

He had never had to work to feel presence before.

Late one evening, as rain drew lines across the windows, Sana turned to him suddenly.

“Do you ever feel like you’re rehearsing?” she asked.

He thought carefully. “Rehearsing what?”

She hesitated. “Life. As if this is... preparation.”

The honesty of the question cut deeper than fear would have.

“Yes,” he said eventually.

“That scares me,” Sana admitted.

“It scares me too,” he replied.

They sat quietly after that, listening to the rain reduce the world to controlled repetition.

Neither of them spoke, but both felt the same unspoken weight:

Whatever this life was, it was approaching resolution.

But not gradually.

Structurally.

Much later that night, Omar stood at the window again.

The city no longer looked like a place expanding outward.

It looked like something folding inward, lines converging toward a point he could not yet see.

For the first time, he wondered—not *if* this life would end—but how abruptly.

And whether, when it did, there would be time for surprise.

The following weeks carried a muted softness, as though the world had lowered its volume deliberately.

Omar continued attending meetings, signing documents, answering questions that required less thinking than alignment. Nothing went wrong. That was the problem. Systems performed exactly as expected. People delivered precisely what they promised. Even disagreements arrived pre-shaped, offering resolution without struggle.

One afternoon, while clearing an old cabinet, Omar found a box he did not remember packing. Inside were objects that should have triggered memory with force—an early company notebook, a faded visitor badge from a conference, a photograph taken during a rushed lunch overseas.

Each item felt accurate.

None felt lived.

He sat on the floor longer than necessary, turning the objects in his hands, waiting for emotion to catch up to information. It never quite did.

That evening, he cooked dinner for the family without announcing it. The children complained playfully about spices being uneven. Sana corrected them gently, then looked at Omar with a small, grateful smile.

For a moment, the room aligned.

Not because it was perfect—but because it was immediate.

Later, while putting the children to bed, the elder one asked a question casually, without intention.

“Papa, where were you before we were here?”

Omar paused.

The answer should have been simple.

He realized then that every version of the truth required explanation instead of memory.

“I was... building something,” he said carefully.

The child accepted this and turned over, sleep arriving without demand.

Omar remained seated longer than required, listening to breathing he no longer needed to monitor.

That night, he wrote again.

Not notes.
Not plans.

Sentences.

Short ones. Observations without purpose.

Time isn’t missing.
It’s compressed.
Nothing feels wrong. Everything feels finished.

He closed the notebook and placed it back where it had been.

The awareness did not disturb his sleep. It accompanied it.

Sometime near dawn, he woke with the distinct sense that he had overslept—though the clock insisted otherwise. He stood at the window, watching the city wake methodically.

Cars moved. Lights switched on. Patterns resumed.

Life continued its correct behaviour.

And yet, standing there, Omar understood something with unsettling clarity:

This life no longer allowed surprises.

It had shifted from experience to execution.

Whatever waited next—whatever boundary approached—it would not announce itself with chaos.

It would arrive cleanly.

Like an ending that believed it had done enough.

***

A few days later, Omar attended a gathering he had agreed to weeks earlier and forgotten entirely. It was the kind of event that once excited him—industry leaders, controlled conversation, polite admiration disguised as inquiry.

He moved through the hall smoothly. Too smoothly.

He answered questions before they were fully asked. Anticipated reactions before they reached faces. At one point, someone laughed at something he said, but Omar realized only afterward that he did not remember choosing the words.

They had come out already formed.

That disturbed him more than failure would have.

On his way out, a journalist stopped him briefly. “Almost two decades of growth,” she said. “What keeps you grounded?”

Omar paused.

The pause felt longer to him than it appeared to her.

“Constraints,” he said finally. “When you design with limits, you don’t drift.”

She nodded, satisfied.

He was not.

On the drive home, city lights streaked by like passing markers on a track. He watched them without attachment, aware that speed no longer registered. Only direction did.

At home, Sana had fallen asleep on the sofa with a book open on her chest. Omar covered her gently with a blanket and sat beside her, watching her breathing settle deeper.

He tried to recall falling in love.

Not facts.
Not milestones.

The sensation.

What returned was not absence, but a neutral correctness—as though love had arrived on schedule and behaved exactly as planned.

That frightened him more than the thought of losing it.

He stayed awake that night, listening to the quiet hum of the city beyond the windows, aware that the feeling he was chasing was no longer memory.

He woke too often in those weeks — not from alarms, not from distress, but because the architecture of his nights had shifted. Sleep no longer reset the day; it stitched days together. He would fall into slumber at the edge of a thought and wake to find that thought had moved forward without him. Sometimes he could reconstruct the motion; often he could not. The sense of being outpaced by clarity gnawed at him in small ways: a sentence finished before he could utter it, a meeting resolved as he entered the room, a child's question answered by habit before he registered the need to ask it.

Routine became a mirror that reflected competence more than feeling. He found comfort in its predictability but also a peculiar hunger for surprise — the kind that did not arrive in headlines or product launches, but in the small, uncatalogued interruptions of life. A neighbor bringing over an unexpected plate of food. A rainstorm that routed traffic differently, forcing him to stand under a stranger's awning and exchange a moment of soft conversation. A child mispronouncing a word and inventing a tiny joke that no strategy meeting could manufacture. Those instances, brief and unremarkable to anyone else, became points of calibration: cheap and fragile proofs that not everything had been folded into the mechanism.

At times he suspected the compression was not the world's doing but his own. He had designed systems to remove friction; perhaps, he worried, he had removed enough of it from himself that the edges of experience rounded off. Where earlier he had noticed the texture of choices — their roughness, their resistance — now choices felt smoothed by process. The result was efficiency; the cost was a blurring of contour. He began to test that hypothesis quietly, deliberately. He would take a route home that added ten minutes to his commute; he would sit with the children for a full story instead of the summary he usually offered; he would let a meeting run an extra five minutes even when he knew the conclusion. The experiments yielded small returns: a laugh that started later and grew longer, a child's hand squeezed rather than neatly arranged, a colleague's idea that surfaced because someone else had time to think it through.

Sana noticed the tests as well. She did not name them for him; she participated in them. She would suggest a walk that took them past a bookshop they rarely entered, or she would insist on a weekend without screens. Sometimes she pressed him gently: "Stay." He would stay, and the act of staying began to accumulate as a practice rather than a concession. It did not fix the sensation entirely — the fold remained — but it made the folds gentler. In those small rebellions against efficiency, he felt less like a machine and more like a person practicing being present.

Friends and colleagues observed shifts in tone but not in fact. Nuclear Technologies continued its carefully measured growth. The pilots widened into several small contracts; metrics improved; the steady drip of adoption continued. Yet outside the office, conversations about him were changing in texture, too. What had once been curiosity hardened into expectation. Where people earlier asked whether he could, they now assumed he would. That assumption mattered; it applied pressure that was not loud but algebraic, the kind that changes equations when you introduce new variables. Omar adapted. He refined thresholds. He learned to say no with the same precision he used for code — concise, defensible, unambiguous.

The paradox was that as the company's footprint widened, his personal footprint shrank. Not in significance, but in elasticity. He was visible in reports and invisible in the messy contours of living. His children loved him with the bluntness of habit; his wife trusted him with a confidence that did not require daily proof. And yet somewhere inside the steady rhythm, a question repeated itself without forming into full speech: What would happen when the architecture he'd designed needed to bend in a way he had not anticipated? He had engineered for failure modes and edge cases, but he had prepared less for surprise that was not technical in nature — for grief, for acute joy, for the sudden irrelevance of a plan.

That question arrived as the faintest of presences at first, a peripheral awareness that made him pause more often. He grew attentive to bodily signals he had previously neglected: a tightness in the chest during a long meeting, a flutter of dizziness when he rose too quickly, an odd heaviness behind his eyes in the late afternoon. He booked check-ups, adjusted his sleep windows, drank more water. These were utilitarian moves, not panics. He preferred to treat uncertainty as a maintenance problem: detect early, mitigate aggressively. This approach calmed him, though it did not erase the sense that something — not necessarily catastrophic, but decisive — lurked outside the predictable envelope.

Conversations with Hazir became less about technical process and more about language. "Do you ever feel," Hazir asked over a shared dinner, "that you are collecting time rather than living it?" Omar considered the phrasing. It had the right shape. "I manage time," he answered. "I do not collect it." Hazir looked at him as if he had missed the point, then softened. "Managing is not the same as inhabiting." The words stayed with Omar. He could not correct them. He could only test them.

So he added small rituals to his days: a single page of writing in the morning, sentences not intended as plans; a hand-drawn map of the week, marking nothing but meals; a deliberate pause at sunset, a time he refused to fill with thought. These acts had no measurable ROI. They were, he told himself, hedges against a life that had become too neatly predictable. They were also, he realized, invitations — token offerings to a future that might still surprise him. Each act felt embarrassingly earnest and yet strangely necessary.

The children's questions grew in different directions. They asked about animals, about machines, about why rain sometimes smelled certain ways. Omar answered with the closest truths he had. Occasionally his answers faltered; sometimes he diverted by asking them what they thought. Those moments opened small doors. He kept returning to one simple approach: ask more than tell. He had designed systems to remove answers; now he used the same principle with his family, cultivating spaces where discovery mattered more than resolution.

And in that cultivate-and-wait practice, he discovered an odd relief. The fold of years, which had once felt like compression into unavoidable outcomes, loosened slightly. It did not unravel. It rebalanced. Instead of feeling pushed toward a single inevitable point, he began to see a spread of adjacent possibilities — muted, modest, human — where surprise could still land.

He did not celebrate this shift. He tracked it in his notebook with the same attention he gave user metrics: a short note, a date, a sentence. The entries were not numerous. They were sincere. When he reread them later, they read like a ledger of small resistances — a record of choices that prioritized presence over performance. It was not triumph. It was practice.

One evening, as rain began to draw thin silver threads across the windows, Omar sat with Sana and the children and watched the droplets collect. The city outside softened into a watercolor of light and distance. Inside, voices rose and fell with the easy rhythm of family, unplanned and utterly messy. He felt an unfamiliar gratitude — not the tidy satisfaction of a checklist completed, but a raw, immediate appreciation for an interruption that had nothing to do with alignment.

He set his notebook aside and reached for his child's small hand. The contact was ordinary in every way. Yet in the steady, unremarkable pressure of that grip he felt the wedge of the fold shift just enough to let a sliver of surprise through. It did not change the architecture of his life. It simply reminded him that architecture could contain rooms for things that had not been scheduled. And that reminder, he knew, might be the most valuable correction of all.

It was signal.

And it was pointing forward, not backward.

****

Chapter 8 – Doubts Inside Happiness

Omar was tying his younger child's shoelaces when the question came.

"Papa," the child said, watching his hands closely, "why do you always do everything so fast?"

Omar paused.

"I don't," he said. "I just don't like repeating things."

The child considered this seriously, then nodded as if that explained something important.

Sana watched from the doorway.

"You still finished before breakfast got cold," she said.

"That's efficiency," Omar replied lightly.

"That's avoidance," she countered, not unkindly.

He looked up at her. "Avoidance of what?"

She didn't answer immediately.

"That pause," she said finally. "You never stay inside it."

Later that day, at the office, Omar noticed the same thing happening again.

A junior manager was explaining a potential risk—slowly, carefully, visibly nervous. Omar listened for less than a minute before interrupting.

"It won't happen," Omar said.

The manager blinked. "Sir, we haven't—"

"I know," Omar continued calmly. "But it won't."

The room went quiet.

Someone cleared their throat. Another person glanced at the projector as if the presentation might rescue them.

"Should we still document the contingency?" someone asked.

Omar nodded. "Yes. For discipline. Not because you'll need it."

After the meeting, Kabir caught up with him in the hallway.

"You've started skipping steps again," Kabir said.

Omar smiled faintly. "I've already walked them."

"That's what you said before Hyderabad," Kabir replied.

Omar stopped walking.

"That's different," he said.

Kabir raised an eyebrow. "Is it?"

***

That night, dinner was louder than usual.

The kids argued about who drank more juice. Sana corrected them. Omar intervened with unnecessary precision, dividing the remaining juice equally, measuring fairness into submission.

Sana watched him do it.

“You know they’d eventually stop fighting without your math,” she said.

“Yes,” Omar replied. “But this is faster.”

She set her fork down. “Do you hear yourself?”

He looked up. “What?”

She shook her head lightly. “You’re treating life like a backlog.”

The words stung—not because they were harsh, but because they were accurate.

After dinner, while washing dishes, Sana spoke again.

“You don’t ask questions anymore.”

“I answer them,” Omar said.

“That’s not the same,” she replied. “You used to wonder out loud with me.”

He dried a plate slowly. “Wondering doesn’t change the outcome.”

She turned to face him. “Since when are outcomes the point?”

He didn’t have a good answer.

That night, Omar woke up thinking someone had called his name.

“Sana?” he whispered.

She didn’t move.

His heart wasn’t racing. His breathing wasn’t shallow. There was no fear—just the uncomfortable sense that he had missed something important.

The next morning, he mentioned it casually.

“I thought I heard something last night,” he said.

Sana glanced up from making tea. “Like a dream?”

“No,” Omar said. “Like a reminder.”

She frowned slightly. “A reminder of what?”

“I don’t know,” he admitted.

That unsettled her more than certainty would have.

***

A few days later, while driving home, Omar stopped at a signal he usually raced through. A man crossed the road slowly, talking to someone on the phone, unconcerned with traffic.

For the first time in years, Omar felt irritation—not at the delay, but at how unnecessary the delay felt.

Then, abruptly, irritation faded.

What replaced it was worse.

Indifference.

He turned the radio off and drove the rest of the way home in silence.

That evening, while lying on the bed with documents spread around him, Sana sat beside him and closed the laptop gently.

"You're finished with today," she said.

"I wasn't done," he replied.

"Yes," she said. "You were."

He studied her face.

"You think something's wrong with me."

"I think something has *completed* too early," she said softly.

That sentence stayed with him long after she fell asleep.

Much later, alone in the living room, Omar spoke aloud—to the empty room, to the night, to whatever might still be listening.

"If this is the best version," he said quietly, "why does it feel like the ending?"

The silence didn't answer.

But it didn't feel empty either.

It felt patient.

***

Omar didn't plan to stay late at the office that evening, but the building felt unusually quiet—almost too quiet. The kind of quiet that carries shape, like someone had wrapped the entire place in insulation. Even the hum of air-conditioning sounded muted, as if it were choosing not to interrupt him.

Most employees had left already. Only a few screens still glowed behind glass-walled rooms, their blue-white reflections splashing across empty chairs. Omar walked past them slowly, not toward anything specific—just moving.

He stopped near the large window overlooking the city. The skyline pulsed with its usual evening rhythm, but something in the motion felt off. He watched a cluster of cars move down a highway. They drifted in perfect unison, maintaining distance too precisely.

Not impossible.

Just unnatural.

He blinked, and the pattern broke—cars resumed their irregular spacing, jolts and hesitations returning as if embarrassed by the moment of symmetry.

His phone buzzed.

A message from Sana:

Dinner is light today. Come home early.

He replied:

Leaving soon.

He didn't leave.

He wandered into the smaller conference room—one with a round table and no screens. It was the room he often used when thinking, not deciding. He sat down and placed both hands flat on the table.

He listened.

Not to sounds.

To absence.

After several minutes, he whispered into the room:

"Something is shifting."

The lights above flickered faintly—not enough to startle, just enough to acknowledge.

Kabir found him there ten minutes later.

"You're still here?" Kabir asked, dropping into a chair across from him.

"You said the same thing last month," Omar replied.

"That's because you forget what time is."

Omar looked at him carefully. "Do you ever feel like time is responding instead of passing?"

Kabir blinked. "Responding to what?"

"To us."

Kabir exhaled heavily. "You're overworked."

"I'm not tired," Omar said calmly.

"That's worse," Kabir muttered. "When you get tired, you stop. When you don't get tired, you drift."

Omar didn't react.

Kabir leaned forward. "Tell me what's going on. Really."

Omar waited before answering.

"There are days when I predict things before, they happen—not because of intuition. Because I *remember* them."

Kabir frowned. “As déjà vu?”

“No. Déjà vu comes with confusion. This comes with certainty. A scene happens, and I think, ‘Of course.’”

Kabir stared, struggling to shape the right response. “That’s not… normal.”

“Nothing in my life has been normal for seventeen years,” Omar said softly.

Kabir opened his mouth, then closed it again.

“What does Sana say?”

“Too much,” Omar replied. “And not enough.”

***

Sana had been patient in ways that made patience look like strength, not compromise. She had watched Omar grow more accomplished, more distant, more precise. She understood parts of him that even he ignored. Their conversations had become intervals of clarity between long stretches of quiet.

But lately, even those intervals had thinned.

Tonight, she waited at home, pacing the living room. The children were asleep, but she kept the hallway light on, a habit from years earlier when Omar returned late too often.

She didn’t feel anxious.

She felt vigilant.

When he finally walked in, she didn’t greet him immediately. She watched him place his keys on the table and exhale in a way that sounded like a decision rather than relief.

"You stayed late," she said.

"Yes."

"You didn't text."

"I thought I did."

She crossed her arms. "You didn't."

He nodded as though confirming a detail rather than apologizing.

Sana approached him slowly.

"Omar," she said softly. "Talk to me."

He looked at her, not evasive, just unaligned.

"I don't know how much of today actually happened," he said.

The sentence hit her harder than she expected.

"Omar..."

"I remember the work," he continued. "I know the outcomes. But I don't remember the feeling of moving through it."

Sana took his hand. "That's not normal."

"Nothing around me feels normal anymore."

"Do you feel unwell? Physically?"

"No."

"Lost?"

"No."

"Then what?" she pressed.

He searched for the word.

“Finished,” he said.

Sana stepped back slightly, as if the word had pushed her.

“Finished with what?”

“With... unfolding. My life is behaving like it already knows the ending.”

She covered her mouth briefly, not with shock but fear.

He continued, voice steady:

“There are moments when I feel like I’m only here to experience the *last chapters* of something already written.”

Sana sat down slowly; breath steady but shallow.

“Do you think you’re dying?” she asked quietly.

“No,” he said. “I think I’m approaching a point.”

“What point?”

“I don’t know.”

***

Later, Sana made tea for both of them—not because they needed it, but because tea marked transitions. It allowed silence to gather without becoming confrontation.

They sat at the small dining table.

Sana held her cup tightly. “I need you to tell me something honestly.”

"Yes."

"Do you feel... disconnected from this family?"

"No," Omar said immediately.

"From me?"

"No."

"From yourself?"

He didn't answer immediately.

Finally: "Sometimes."

Sana swallowed hard. "Describe it."

"I feel like I'm watching myself behave correctly," Omar said. "Like I'm fulfilling something. But I don't feel the weight of choosing it."

She whispered, "That's terrifying."

"It feels clean," he corrected.

She shook her head. "Clean is not always good, Omar. Clean can be empty."

He looked down at his hands.

"That's the part I don't understand," he said quietly.

Two days later, something small broke the pattern.

Omar woke before dawn and found his reflection in the bathroom mirror... unfamiliar. Not older. Not changed. Just unfamiliar, as though he had seen the reflection too many times and it had lost its connection to him.

He leaned closer.

His eyes did not feel like the ones that had lived this life. They looked like they had *inherited* it.

He touched the glass lightly.

"What are you preparing me for?" he whispered.

***

That morning, Sana insisted they walk to the nearby park. She held his hand tightly, not romantically but firmly, as though grounding him by force.

"At least pretend you're here," she said.

"I am here."

"Prove it."

"How?"

"Talk about something small."

He considered. "The grass is overwatered."

"Try again."

"The air smells like rain."

"One more."

He paused longer this time.

"I want to hear your voice more," he said softly.

Sana's expression softened painfully. "Then don't drift."

"I don't know how to stop drifting," he admitted.

She breathed out slowly. "Then I'll hold you still."

"Until when?"

"Until you stop feeling finished."

He nodded gratefully.

But deep down, he feared that point wouldn't return.

***

At the office the following week, an unusual meeting took place—one that did not appear on the calendar.

Omar walked into a small conference room expecting a routine check-in. Instead, three board members sat waiting for him, posture formal.

"We want to discuss transition plans," one said.

Omar raised an eyebrow. "Transition to what?"

"A reduced-director model," another said. "The company is too dependent on your forecasting."

"That's a problem?" Omar asked.

"It's a risk," the third replied. "If anything happens to you—"

Omar froze at the phrasing.

"If anything happens to me," he repeated slowly.

"Yes," the board member said. "Your predictions are accurate. But they are too accurate. Teams rely on your instincts over their own work. If you're unavailable, the entire structure may collapse."

Omar leaned back. "You think I'm fragile."

"We think the system is," she corrected.

For the first time, Omar felt... alignment.

They were right.

He *was* approaching something.

Something final.

He dismissed the meeting gently and walked out, pulse steady but mind whispering:

They saw it too.

***

That evening, when he returned home, Sana met him at the door.

"How was the day?"

"Confirming," he said.

They sat on the sofa.

"Omar," she said softly, "look at me."

He did.

"You think something is coming, don't you?"

"Yes."

"You think it's soon?"

"Yes."

She held his face with both hands. "Is it bad?"

He shook his head gently. "I don't think it's bad. I think it's precise."

Sana closed her eyes. "I don't want precise. I want messy. I want unpredictable."

"I know," he whispered. "I do too."

Night approached quietly. Omar walked to the children's room and watched them sleep—breathing evenly, curled in familiar positions. For the first time in a long while, he felt emotion arrive unfiltered. Raw. Human.

He sat on the floor beside their beds and whispered:

"I don't know how long this lasts. But I'm here now."

He remained there until his legs went numb.

***

When he returned to his own room, Sana was sitting upright on the bed, looking troubled but composed.

"Omar," she said softly, "if you feel something coming... promise me you won't walk into it alone."

He approached her slowly.

"I'm not walking into it," he said.

"Then what?"

"It's walking toward me."

She covered her mouth, tears threatening.

"Please don't talk like that."

He gently held her hand.

"It's not fear," he said. "It's recognition."

She shook her head. "You're scaring me."

"I'm scaring myself," he admitted.

He looked around the room, at the lamp, the curtains, the familiar shadows.

Everything felt... temporary.

Like the final scene before a transition.

He whispered:

“Sana... I think the story is shortening.”

Before sleep, he stared at the ceiling and felt something he had not felt in years:

A countdown.

Not numbered.
Not rushed.

Just present.

Like a pressure behind glass.

Waiting.

He began counting small things he could still measure. Not tasks, not achievements—those had become trivial—but intervals: the seconds it took a child to fall asleep after a story, the length of a neighbor’s greeting, the pause between a question and the answer it provoked. They were petty audits, almost superstitious, but they gave him a way to hold the present in his hands. If the world had begun to behave as though its chapters were already written, then these intervals were bookmarks he could place between pages.

Days folded into a steady pattern of attention and half-attention. Mornings he spent like a man running checks—meetings, strategy, a brief review of support metrics—followed by afternoons where he tried deliberately to be unmechanical: an unstructured conversation with a junior engineer about music, a slow cup of tea with Kabir where the talk avoided deadlines, a drive with Sana that took a longer route home and stopped for a pastry neither of them needed. These interruptions did not fix anything, but they eroded the crisp edges of his certainties enough to let something unquantified slip through.

At work the board's quiet concern settled like a second skin. People adjusted their behaviors: junior leads documented decisions more thoroughly, teams rehearsed contingency plans instead of relying on instinct, and Omar found himself watching the office through the same clinical attention he gave systems. He noticed who looked to him first, whose hands trembled when he interrupted, whose proposals suddenly asked for his imprimatur before being released. The pattern was less flattering when he saw it mapped: his presence simplified other people's mental load to the point of dependency. That realization arrived without drama, but it left a residue—an awkward, patient grief for the autonomy he had accidentally taken away.

Sana met him in those evenings like a lighthouse—steady, warm, demanding nothing more than honesty. She did not dramatize his observations; she catalogued them. "If you are becoming the axis," she said once, "then people will spin around you until you ask them not to." Her voice was matter-of-fact, not reproachful. Her clarity frightened him more than any external critique. He responded by being transparent in small things: sharing board notes, inviting a junior to present to the leadership team without his edit, refusing to answer questions in meetings that he could assign to others. Each act felt cumbersome at first, then necessary. He realized control needed to be redistributed like currency—spent, invested, tracked.

Still, the private sensations did not relent. He woke sometimes in the night hearing his own voice deliver a sentence he had not yet thought, felt the certainty of decisions before the meetings began, and experienced the odd phenomenon of time compressing events into conclusions he knew would be true. It was not prescience; it was more like a misplaced memory of things not yet lived. The sensation eroded spontaneity. He missed the clumsy, inefficient moments that once produced small delights precisely because they were accidental.

He started writing differently. The sentences became shorter, less strategic, more like logs—"Saw Nur smile at breakfast. Forgot to ask him about school project." "Listened to Kabir rant. Did not correct." The entries were not meant for anyone; they were a grammar exercise in being present. Sometimes the act of writing forced his mind to linger on a detail long enough for warmth to form around it. Other times the notes read back as inventory, sterile and unemotional, which terrified him more than the absence of feeling.

Friends noticed the change and treated it as a curiosity rather than an emergency. Majid laughed and called him "CEO of Time" in a text that was affectionate but faintly mocking. Hazir visited and sat with him in silence long enough for both of them to notice that silence had shifted its meaning. "You're more precise," Hazir observed. "But precision only cares about edges." Omar did not argue. He recorded the line in his notebook later and underlined it.

One evening, after putting the children to bed, they all sat at the table and ate in a quiet choreography as though the family itself were an apparatus to be tended. Conversation was minimal; presence was practiced. Sana reached across the table and squeezed his hand with firm, ordinary pressure, then let go. The contact felt like a tether rather than a rescue. He held onto it gratefully because it was tangible: a human measure against the abstract sensation that increasingly dominated his days.

He also sought medical reassurance—tests, a thorough check-up, nothing sensational to report. The doctors smiled at him with clinical kindness and recommended adjustments that were sensible but unalarming: sleep hygiene, reduced screen time, occasional monitoring. The practical advice should have eased his mind. It did not. The doctors' uncertainty in the face of his described experience was itself unsettling; their language was necessarily conservative—"idiopathic," "monitor," "follow up"—and the vagueness echoed the one thing he feared: indifference.

A quiet calendar entry appeared one Sunday: "Write a letter." He did not specify to whom. The act surprised him. He sat at the same table where he logged metrics and drafted roadmaps, and he wrote sentences that were not for strategy but for companions, small notes that affirmed ordinary things: "You were here; you did this." He sealed the folded paper into an envelope and left it on the dining table where Sana would find it later. Doing it felt childish and consequential at once, a small investment in the practice of memory.

As the weeks moved, he developed a ritual—no grand gestures, nothing dramatic—simply a discipline of noticing. He would pause deliberately three times a day and catalog aloud one thing he liked about the moment: the sound of the kettle, the way sunlight struck the dining table, his child's small predictable laugh. Sometimes Sana joined. Sometimes she did not. The practice did not cure the sensation of acceleration, but it created a lattice through which days could be threaded and refracted, so that even if time continued to fold, there would be visible seams.

One afternoon, while reviewing a product demo, he found himself smiling at a bug report that read, in a user's voice, "The app forgot my name, but I liked that it let me start again." He printed the comment and pinned it near his monitor. The note was small, unremarkable, and suddenly precious. It reminded him that systems can forget—and that forgetting can sometimes be the space where new things begin. It was not a revelation; it was a small permission to be less certain.

He did not stop feeling the pressure. He learned to sit with it without treating it as an enemy. In that accommodation there was an odd relief: if the future was precise, then making room for the unpredictable became, itself, a practice. He kept the notebook, the short sentences, the paused conversations; he kept the rituals and the envelopes. He kept saying yes to the messy interruptions and no to the siren calls of spectacle. The balance was fragile, imperfect, and quietly maintained.

On certain nights, when the house settled and the city outside softened to a distant pulse, he would wake with the faint sense that something was drawing near. But the sensation had changed: it no longer felt like a countdown only he could hear. Sometimes, in the light between sleep and wakefulness, Sana's hand would find his, steady and warm, and he would let the present hold him for a little while longer. He could not promise that the fold would loosen entirely. He could promise, however, that he would try to keep small things honest—little bookmarks in the book of days—so that if the story shortened, moments would still be there to meet it.

*****

Chapter 9 – Seventeen Years Complete

Omar woke before dawn.

Not abruptly. Not from a dream.
He simply opened his eyes and found the room watching him.

The ceiling fan rotated in a steady rhythm, its hum softer than usual, as if considerate. The window was still dark, but the air carried the faint hint of morning—cool, slow-moving, alive in a way the rest of the world hadn't felt for months.

He shifted slightly and realized Sana was awake beside him.

She wasn't looking at him, not yet. She stared toward the far corner of the room, breathing evenly but vigilantly, as though the night had been spent in conversation with her own fears.

"You didn't sleep," Omar said quietly.

She turned her head, offering a small, tired smile.
"You didn't drift."

He exhaled softly. "Not yet."

Sana studied his face. "Does today feel different?"

Omar didn't answer immediately.

"Yes," he said.

“How?”

“Like a decision.”

Sana closed her eyes briefly. “Yours? Or something else’s?”

“I’m not sure anymore.”

She took his hand beneath the blanket. Her fingers were warm, steady, grounding.

“Stay with us today,” she said. “Whatever else is moving… let it wait.”

Omar nodded. “I will.”

He meant it.
He believed it.
He hoped it.

***

The morning unfolded with deliberate normalcy.

Sana cooked breakfast, insisting on doing everything herself despite Omar offering repeatedly to help. She said she wanted “control of the kitchen.” He understood what she meant: she wanted grounding, tasks that behaved predictably.

The children ran around half-dressed, arguing about a pencil box and who had hidden it. Their voices overlapped, collided, resolved. Omar watched them with an intensity that felt unfamiliar—not admiration, not nostalgia.

Presence.

Full presence.

“Papa, tell him to stop!” the younger one shouted.

Omar stepped into the argument with exaggerated seriousness, crouching to their level.

“Whoever returns the pencil box first,” he announced, “gets to choose dessert tonight.”

Both children froze.

“Dessert?” the older one asked.

“Yes,” Omar said. “Anything that doesn’t require fire or refrigeration.”

They exchanged a look and dashed off toward the bedroom, laughter trailing behind them.

Sana, watching from the kitchen, smiled with an expression that was almost painful.

“You’re here,” she whispered to herself.

Omar heard her.

“Yes,” he said.

But the truth was more complicated.

He was here—fully, intensely—but only because something inside him knew this presence would not repeat.

***

By mid-morning, he took a walk alone.

Just around the block.
Just to breathe.

He didn’t tell Sana, but she watched him from the window until he disappeared from sight.

The neighborhood was ordinary—quiet shops, narrow footpaths, families starting their routines. Omar walked slowly, slower than he usually allowed himself. His feet felt heavier, aware. The ground beneath him felt more textured, as if refusing to be dismissed as background.

He stopped near a small tea stall.

The vendor smiled. "Long time, sir."

"Has it been?" Omar asked.

"Yes," the man laughed. "Many months. Maybe more. You always ordered chai without sugar."

Omar hesitated.
That order felt like it belonged to a different version of him.

"Today with sugar," he said.

The vendor raised an eyebrow. "Changing rules?"

"Maybe returning to some."

When Omar took the first sip, the sweetness startled him—not because of the taste, but because he remembered sweetness so clearly it felt unfamiliar.

"How old are you now, sir?" the vendor asked casually.

Omar paused.

It was a harmless question.
Harmless, until he tried to answer it.

"Thirty-eight," he said finally.

The vendor nodded. “Good age. Most people start living properly by then.”

Omar smiled politely, but something in his chest tightened.

Thirty-eight.

A full life behind him.
And yet, his body felt twenty.
His mind felt ageless.
His memories felt borrowed.

He finished the tea and walked away.

Behind him, the vendor watched with a puzzled expression—as though he sensed something Omar hadn’t said aloud.

When he returned home, Sana was sitting on the sofa, pretending to read. She closed the book immediately.

“You were gone longer than I expected.”

“I walked slower than I expected,” Omar replied.

She studied him carefully. “Are you okay?”

“Yes.”

“Are you telling me the truth?”

“Yes,” he said again.

She didn’t look convinced, but she didn’t push.

“Come,” she said softly. “Stay with us.”

***

The afternoon passed in fragments of domesticity.

Helping with homework.
Answering work calls he tried to avoid.
Fixing a loose cupboard hinge.
Listening to Sana remind the children about finishing their meals.

It was a normal day.

Painfully normal.

And that was what made it so strange.

Every moment arrived fully formed, polished, complete. There were no rough edges, no spontaneous delights, no unpredictable laughter. Everything felt like a memory being replayed rather than an event unfolding.

At one point, while helping his daughter with a school assignment, Omar paused mid-sentence.

She noticed. "Papa?"

"I just—" He blinked. "I felt like we already had this conversation."

She giggled. "We do homework *every day*."

"No," he said gently. "This exact moment."

She tilted her head. "Like magic?"

"Yes," he said. "Something like that."

She returned to her writing, unfazed.

Omar did not.

Around sunset, the house shifted into evening rhythm.
Lights softened.

Phones were set aside.
Dinner simmered quietly on the stove.

Omar stood at the balcony again, feeling the air change temperature.

Sana joined him.

"Do you feel it?" she asked.

He didn't ask what she meant.

"Yes."

"Is it getting closer?"

"Yes."

She swallowed. "Can you stop it?"

"No."

"Can I help?"

He looked at her.

"You're helping already," he said softly. "You're the reason I'm not afraid."

Her eyes filled—but tears didn't fall.

"Promise me something," she said.

"When it comes, don't go alone."

He hesitated.

"I will try," he said.

That was the most honest promise he could give.

Night approached slowly.

The children went to bed with their usual rituals—negotiations for one more story, arguments about who brushed their teeth first, too much energy compressed into too few minutes.

Omar kissed their foreheads, lingering longer than usual.

"You're acting weird," the older one whispered.

Omar smiled. "I'm acting grateful."

"Weird," the child repeated, satisfied.

He sat by their bedside until both children drifted into soft breathing.

Then he remained sitting.
Just listening.
Just existing.

It felt like a privilege he had forgotten he possessed.

***

When he stepped into the hallway, he found Sana waiting near the doorway, leaning against the wall.

"Come here," she said.

He walked toward her, and she wrapped her arms around him tightly—so tightly it felt like she was trying to hold him inside time.

"I don't want this to be the last peaceful day," she whispered.

"It won't be," he said.

But he didn't know.

And she knew he didn't know.

"What if tomorrow changes everything?" she asked.

Omar rested his forehead against hers.

"Then let today be enough."

She closed her eyes slowly, taking in his warmth as though memorizing it.

"Is it enough for you?" she asked.

Omar thought deeply.

"Yes," he said. "Today is enough."

It was the first time in years he genuinely felt that.

But the truth beneath it—the truth that scared him—was this:

Today felt like everything.

Everything complete.

Everything concluded.

Everything waiting.

***

As he lay down that night, the air felt heavier, as if the room was bracing for something. The ceiling fan spun in a rhythm that sounded more deliberate than mechanical.

Sana touched his arm lightly. "Omar?"

"Yes."

"Stay with me tomorrow."

"I will."

He meant it.

But somewhere inside him—somewhere older than memory—he understood:

Tomorrow was not his to control.

It was coming toward him already.

***

And that realization did not frighten him.
It softened him.

It felt as if time had shifted from a river he walked beside to a tide that had begun moving around him—slow, deliberate, patient. Not dragging him. Not pulling him. Simply carrying him with the quiet certainty of something long decided.

He lay there in the dim light of the bedroom, Sana breathing evenly beside him, the rhythm of her sleep steady and familiar. Her warmth grounded him, anchoring him to the bed, to the room, to this moment. But even this closeness, this intimacy carved by years of shared life, felt like something he was holding gently rather than gripping tightly.

A breeze slipped through the half-open window, lifting the edge of the curtain with a whisper-soft sway. Omar watched it move, watched the thin fabric flutter like it was answering a call from somewhere outside the room. It seemed to respond to something he could not hear.

He breathed out slowly, letting the quiet settle over him.

It was not a heavy quiet.
Not a quiet of endings or dread.
It was a quiet of acceptance—like standing on a shoreline and watching a distant light approach across calm water.

He felt time reorganizing itself, smoothing out its inconsistencies, gathering itself into one continuous line that pointed forward. For seventeen years, life had flowed like a series of sharp moments—victories, decisions, reflections, regrets. But now everything felt level, balanced, almost too perfect in its symmetry.

Moments that once carried weight now passed lightly, as though time were clearing space for something that required all of him.

He turned slightly and looked at Sana's face in the pale light. She seemed at peace, unaware of the shift happening inside him, unaware of the invisible boundary drawing closer with each breath he took. He wanted to memorize her expression—not in panic, not in desperation, but in gratitude. As if he were preparing to carry her face into some place that memory alone might not reach.

He reached out lightly, brushing a strand of hair away from her forehead.

She stirred, murmured something unintelligible, then settled again.
Her warmth reassured him.

But reassurance did not erase truth.

The truth moved through him like a second heartbeat—quiet, rhythmic, unhurried.

He wasn't walking into tomorrow, he realized.
Tomorrow was walking into him.

Like an inevitable guest.
Like weather.
Like a conclusion written long before the pages that led to it.

And so he allowed his eyes to close, not in surrender, but in a gentle alignment with whatever waited just beyond the horizon of sleep. The night wrapped around him—not as darkness, but as a calm transition, a soft corridor through which the future approached on its own terms.

He breathed once more, deeply.

Tomorrow would come.

And he would meet it.
Not as its master.
Not as its victim.

But as the one it had been moving toward all along.

***

Morning did not break suddenly.
It drifted in—like a light warming behind a thin curtain, as if the world had decided not to startle anything awake.

Omar stirred before the alarm. He lay quiet for a long while, feeling the morning settle around him. He listened to the faint sounds of life outside their window: a street vendor's distant call, the rumble of a delivery truck, a woman sweeping the pavement below. The rhythm of these noises felt unusually harmonious, like an orchestra warming up for a final performance.

He sat up carefully, not to disturb Sana, but she opened her eyes the moment the mattress shifted.

“You’re up early,” she murmured.

“I think the morning came early,” he said, his voice softer than he intended.

She reached out, letting her hand rest briefly on his arm. “Stay home today.”

The words were simple, but the plea beneath them trembled.

He didn’t answer yet. Instead, he stood and walked to the window, pulling the curtains aside. The sky was washed in pale gold—more muted than sunrise, more deliberate, as if the day itself was choosing a slower transition.

“Look at the light,” he said. “It doesn’t feel rushed.”

Sana sat up too, wrapping the blanket around her shoulders. “It feels like it’s waiting.”

Omar turned toward her. Their eyes held.

“It is,” he said. “And it’s waiting for me.”

She closed her eyes, pained by the truth she had already sensed.

They prepared breakfast together—not like a routine, but like a ritual. Every movement felt intentional: the clink of cups, the simmer of tea, the quiet tap of spoons against bowls. The children’s chatter filled the kitchen as if they were trying to anchor the morning in normalcy.

“Papa, can we go to the park after school?” the younger one asked.

“Yes,” Omar said immediately.

Sana’s eyes flicked toward him, but she said nothing.

The older child tugged at his sleeve. “And can we get ice cream?”

“We’ll get two,” Omar replied.

“Papa, that’s too much!”

“That’s why it’s perfect.”

The children giggled, and Sana turned away toward the sink, blinking rapidly.

Omar watched her shoulders.

He saw the trembling she was trying to hide.

He placed a hand gently on her back.

“I’m here,” he whispered.

She didn’t turn.

“I know,” she whispered back. “I just don’t know for how long.”

Omar exhaled softly. “Neither do I.”

***

After breakfast, he helped the children tie their shoelaces, fix their collars, pack their bags—small tasks he had done countless times, but today he felt the texture of each one. He noticed the slight fraying at the edge of a strap, the faint smell of crayons inside a pencil box, the warmth of tiny hands clutching his own.

It all felt amplified.

Not as a warning.

As a farewell gesture the world itself was giving him.

When the school bus arrived, the children hugged him quickly—routine, rushed—but he held them a little longer.

"Papa, why are you hugging like that?" the younger one asked.

"Just saving the warmth," he smiled.

"For what?"

"For later."

They didn't understand, and he was grateful they didn't.

When the door closed behind them, the apartment felt too quiet. Sana leaned against the wall near the shoe rack, arms folded, gaze lowered. Omar approached her slowly.

"Talk to me," she said, her voice firm but breaking.

"What do you want to know?"

"Everything you're not saying."

He hesitated. "I feel like... like the world has reached a conclusion about me."

“A conclusion?” She stepped closer. “What kind?”

“A structural one. I’ve been moving through something designed, and now... the design is ending.”

Her breath shuddered. “Don’t talk like that.”

“It’s the truth.”

“If today is dangerous,” she said, “then don’t go out.”

“It’s not danger,” he replied softly. “It’s arrival.”

“Omar—”

“It will come either way,” he said. “Here or outside. With you watching or not.”

Tears welled in her eyes. “Then why not stay with me when it happens?”

He cupped her face gently. “Because I don’t want you to see it.”

She pulled his hand down, gripping it tightly. “But I want to see you. I want you with me.”

He held her close, breathing slowly, memorizing the scent of her hair, the warmth of her neck, the slight tremble in her fingers.

“I’m not leaving you,” he said. “I’m being taken.”

“By what?”

He hesitated before answering.

“By the story.”

***

Late morning arrived like a soft turning of a page.

Omar walked toward the door, moving as though the air had thickened around him, making each step weightier, more deliberate. Sana followed him, refusing to let distance form.

"Omar," she said, catching his arm, "what if you don't answer this time? What if you break the pattern?"

"Patterns break themselves," he replied. "Not us."

She shook her head violently. "Stop talking in riddles. Just say you'll be careful."

"I will."

"Say you'll come back."

He looked at her with an expression she had never seen on him before—tenderness mixed with inevitability.

"I will come back," he said, "but not in the way either of us expects."

Her breath hitched.

He stepped away gently.

"Stay here," he said.

"No," she whispered. "Stay here with me."

He opened the door slowly.

A soft draft entered the room, carrying with it a faint, unfamiliar stillness.

"Omar..." she whispered again.

He managed a small smile.

"Whatever happens," he said, "happens at the end of the day—not at the beginning."

And with that, he stepped out, the door closing with a soft click that felt too final for such a small sound.

The hallway felt oddly bright, the lights humming with steady precision. Omar pressed the elevator button, and when the doors opened, he hesitated—not in fear, but in acknowledgment.

The elevator waited like a sentence paused.

He stepped inside.

As the doors slid shut, he felt it:

The world aligning itself.
The quiet forming structure.
The ending beginning its approach.

He didn't resist it.

He simply breathed.

And the elevator descended into the day that had already chosen him.

*****

Chapter 10 – Omelette and Paratha

The morning light came in softly—too softly—spreading across the room in a diluted gold that felt more like a memory than sunlight. Omar lay awake, not from restlessness but from an unusual clarity, a sense that the day around him had leaned closer, waiting for him to acknowledge it.

He didn't move at first.

He listened.

The faint hum of the ceiling fan.
The slow breathing of Sana beside him.
The distant bark of a dog in the street.
The world, existing patiently.

Sana stirred before opening her eyes. She shifted closer, her forehead brushing his shoulder.

"You're quiet," she whispered.

"I'm thinking," he said.

"About what?"

He paused. "How today feels."

Sana didn't ask for an explanation. She simply nodded, as if she already understood the weight behind the words. She rested her hand over his chest, feeling the measured rhythm of his breathing.

"Stay close," she murmured.

"I will."

The children's voices filled the apartment a short while later—alive, chaotic, oblivious to any tension woven into the atmosphere. Omar joined them at the table, watching the ordinary morning unfold with gentle astonishment.

His daughter ran up to him holding a half-finished drawing.

"Look, Papa!" she said proudly. "I made a garden."

He took the paper carefully. "It's beautiful."

"It's not done yet," she added. "But I wanted to show you before I forget."

"Why before you forget?" Omar asked.

"Because sometimes I forget things if I don't show them fast," she explained. "Like dreams."

The word landed softly in his mind.

Dreams.

He nodded. "Then thank you for showing me."

His son tugged at his sleeve. "Papa, can I tell you something?"

"Always."

The boy whispered, "Today feels funny. Like the air is slow."

Omar froze for a moment—not visibly, but internally—as if something had struck a familiar chord.

He placed a hand gently on the boy's head. "Maybe the day is thinking," he said.

The boy laughed. “Days can’t think!”

“Some can,” Omar said quietly.

Sana looked at him then, really looked. Her eyes searched his face for answers she feared existed.

But she didn’t ask—not yet.

***

After breakfast, the children left for school with their usual energy. Omar stayed at the doorway longer than necessary, watching the rickshaw disappear around the bend. When he finally turned back inside, Sana was waiting near the dining table, hands clasped.

“Tell me honestly,” she said. “Do you feel something changing?”

“Yes.”

Her breath wavered. “Is it close?”

“Yes.”

She stepped forward. “Can it be interrupted?”

“No.”

“Can you avoid it?”

“No.”

“Can you face it?”

He hesitated, then said, “I think I already am.”

Sana closed her eyes tightly, gripping the edge of the chair until her knuckles whitened. “Then let me face it with you.”

Omar touched her hand gently. "You're already doing that."

They spent the late morning completing small, quiet tasks—tidying the living room, watering plants, folding clothes that didn't need folding. There was no urgency in their movements, only an unspoken intention: to stay close, to remain occupied enough to avoid drowning in the weight of unasked questions.

At noon, Sana suggested a walk.

"Let's get out of the house," she said softly.

Omar agreed.

The streets were calm. Dust rose lightly beneath their steps. A group of schoolchildren passed by, laughing loudly as though the world had made itself entirely for their joy.

Omar watched them pass.

"Do you ever think," he said, "that some days feel like someone else is turning the pages?"

Sana looked at him sharply. "What does that mean?"

"It means the day feels arranged."

"Arranged for what?"

"I don't know," he said. "But everything feels... aligned."

They walked without holding hands—not out of distance, but because both of them kept their arms close, as if anchoring themselves to their own bodies.

At the park, they sat on a bench beneath a neem tree. Children played a little further away, their movements indistinct, almost blurred against the stillness of the air.

Sana finally broke the silence.

"Whatever happens," she said, "stay aware of me. Don't slip away inside yourself."

"I won't," Omar said.

"You promise?"

"Yes. I promise."

She leaned against him, resting her head on his shoulder, and he wrapped an arm around her, feeling how perfectly she fit against him—how this moment felt like something carved out intentionally, delicately.

As if the world wanted them to hold it before letting anything else happen.

***

Evening drifted in slowly.
Dinner was simple.
The children were cheerful.
Life behaved like it always had.

But beneath it all, the air thickened.

Omar felt it in the way the ceiling fan seemed too quiet.
In the way the shadows stretched a little longer than usual.
In the way Sana looked at him when she thought he wasn't watching.

After putting the children to sleep, they returned to the living room, where the soft yellow lamp cast a warm glow on the walls. Omar stood near the window, hands resting in his pockets.

Sana approached him without a word.

“Is it tonight?” she asked.

Omar looked out at the city lights.

“Yes.”

She exhaled shakily, but no tears fell. She had passed the stage of tears. Now there was only acceptance—and fear hidden beneath it like a second heartbeat.

“Then stay with me,” she whispered.

He turned and held her, slowly, gently, fully.

“I’m here,” he said.

And for the first time in weeks, he felt completely present—no drifting, no distance, no quiet internal pulling.

Tonight belonged to them.

The last untouched moment before the world finally revealed what it had been preparing all along.

They stayed like that for a long time, neither speaking nor moving, as though motion itself might cause the fragile balance around them to crack. Sana’s breath warmed the side of his neck. Omar felt every rise and fall of her chest, each breath echoing against the rhythm of his own.

Eventually, Sana shifted slightly, her hands sliding down to hold his arms—firm, steady, unwilling to let him drift away even for a second.

“Sit with me,” she said quietly.

He nodded.

They sat on the floor beside the window, legs folded, shoulders touching. The room felt grounded in a way Omar hadn’t experienced in years. Outside, the city hummed softly; the faint glow of streetlights filtered through the curtains and settled around them like a thin, trembling halo.

Sana traced a slow circle on the back of his hand with her thumb. She wasn’t searching for words; she was searching for courage.

“Do you remember,” she began softly, “when we were first together? How unsure we were?”

“Yes.”

“You were quieter than now.”

“I was afraid,” Omar admitted. “Afraid of wanting too much.”

“And now?”

He exhaled. “I’m afraid of leaving too much behind.”

She swallowed hard. “Then don’t leave.”

He turned slightly, touching his forehead to hers. “If I could choose,” he said, “I would choose to stay. Here. Like this.”

“But something is calling,” she said.

“Yes.”

“And you don’t know what it is.”

“No.”
He paused. “I only know it’s close.”

Sana’s fingers tightened around his. “I hate it,” she whispered. “Not because I don’t understand—but because I do.”

They fell quiet again, but it wasn’t a frightened silence. It was intimate. Heavy. A silence shaped by years of partnership, by shared burdens and private victories, by two people who had spent a lifetime learning how to exist alongside each other.

At one point, Sana leaned her head on his shoulder. “Can I ask you something?”

“Anything.”

“Do you feel regret?”

He shook his head slowly. “No. I only feel... unfinished.”

She nodded—once, sharply, almost defiantly. “Then promise me you’ll finish something tonight.”

“What?”

“Being here,” she said. “Fully. Not thinking beyond this moment.”

He took a slow breath. “I promise.”

The room seemed to breathe with them, the walls softer, the shadows calmer, as if even the world paused out of respect.

And in that pause, in that shared stillness, Omar felt something rare—
A moment that held itself open, wide and tender, waiting to be filled with whatever remained of them.

***

Night deepened gradually, like ink thinning itself across the sky. The city outside softened into a quiet glow, its lights turning into small trembling dots suspended between darkness and distance. Inside the apartment, the world shrank to the warm circle of space Omar and Sana occupied on the bedroom floor.

They didn't move at first. They didn't speak.
They simply existed in the same breath.

The stillness between them was no longer tense—it was tender, fragile, full of meaning neither of them dared to label out loud.

Finally, Sana shifted slightly.

"Come lie down," she whispered.

They moved to the bed, slow and deliberate, as though every movement might change something inside the fabric of the night. Omar lay back, Sana resting against him, her head on his chest, listening to his heart with an attention that bordered on desperation.

"Your heartbeat is steady," she murmured.

"It's holding the moment," he said softly.

She placed her hand over his heart, fingers spread.
"Hold it longer."

"I will."

And for a while—maybe minutes, maybe hours—they stayed like that, listening to each other breathe, letting the night move around them without rushing it.

But time, even softened, eventually insisted on movement.

Omar felt it first—not a shock, not a warning, but a shift. A quiet tightening inside his ribs, as if the rhythm of the world had flickered. As if the edges of the night had begun folding inward.

He sat up slowly.

Sana rose with him immediately. She could feel the change, even if she didn't see it.

"What is it?" she asked.

Omar looked around the room—the lamp, the curtain, the faint outline of the cupboard, the shadow of their joined hands on the wall.

"It's close," he said.

Sana's breath shuddered. "How close?"

"Tonight."

She closed her eyes. "So this is the last night."

"No," he said. "It's the last moment before the moment."

She didn't fully understand. She didn't need to.

"Omar," she whispered, trembling, "just come to bed. Just lie down. Just be here."

He nodded, and they lay down again, facing each other now.

Sana held his wrist lightly, as if feeling the pulse itself would anchor him to her.

“Talk to me,” she said.

“About what?”

“About anything. Something that keeps you here.”

He thought for a long moment.

“I used to imagine,” he said quietly, “that success would feel like escape.”

“And did it?”

“No. It felt like distance.”

She moved closer. “From what?”

“From myself. From time. From”—he touched her cheek gently— “you.”

Tears welled in her eyes, falling quietly onto the pillow. “But you came back.”

“Yes,” he said. “At the end, everything comes back to where it began.”

Sana pressed her forehead to his. “Stay with me. Whatever happens, stay.”

“I will stay as long as I can.”

She kissed him softly—once, lightly, trembling. “That’s all I ask.”

***

It was a little past midnight when the call came.

Omar's phone buzzed on the bedside table; its vibration sharp in the quiet room. He didn't reach for it. Sana looked at him, shaking her head slowly.

"Don't answer."

He didn't.

But the second call came immediately after.

Again, he let it ring.

The third call didn't stop.
It buzzed continuously, insistent, urgent.

Sana grabbed it and saw the caller's name:
Kabir — Emergency

Her heart dropped.

"Omar..." she whispered. "Something's wrong."

Omar looked at the phone—not surprised, not alarmed.
He simply knew.

"It's time," he said.

Sana covered her mouth, holding back a sound between a sob and a plea. "Don't go."

But Omar leaned forward, pressing his forehead to hers.

"I have to stand where the story ends," he whispered. "If I hide, it will still come."

Tears fell freely now. "Then let me come with you."

"No," he said gently. "You stay here. With me. Until I return in the way I'm meant to."

Sana's voice broke. "You won't come back."

"Yes," he said softly. "Just not the way you expect."

***

He left the apartment with her standing in the doorway, her hand covering her mouth, eyes filled with desperate silence. They didn't hug again. They didn't kiss. They didn't speak. Everything between them had already been said.

Omar stepped into the hallway, feeling the cold air gather around him like an invisible cloak.
He pressed the elevator button.

Just before the doors closed, Sana whispered through the narrow opening:

"I love you."

Omar's lips curved gently.

"I love you too."

The elevator closed between them.

The drive to the office was quiet. Too quiet. The roads were clear, the lights green, the world strangely cooperative—as if clearing the path for him, guiding him toward the inevitable.

When he stepped from the car, the air felt heavier, as though it carried the weight of something waiting just beyond sight.

He entered the building.

The lobby lights were dim.
The security guard nodded nervously.
The elevator doors opened without hesitation.

Omar stepped inside.

His reflection in the stainless-steel walls looked back at him—not young, not old, not afraid.

Just ready.

***

When the elevator opened onto the sixth floor, the world instantly sharpened.

A sound.
A shout.
A figure turning.
A glint of metal.
A flash.

The first shot tore through the hallway.
Omar felt the impact like a sudden force pushing him backward—not sharp pain, just violent pressure.

He staggered.
Another blast shook the air.
His vision blurred, then narrowed.

He collapsed onto one knee, palm hitting the cold floor.

Voices erupted.
Footsteps thundered.
Someone screamed his name.

And then—

Everything fractured.

Not into chaos.
Into stillness.

The world dimmed.
His breath stuttered.
Faces bent over him.
A siren wailed, distant but urgent.

His hearing faded.
His vision tunnelled.

Someone lifted him.
Hands pressed to his wound.
Voices said, “Stay with us! Stay awake!”
A stretcher rolled beneath him.

Lights blurred above him in rapid succession.

A hospital ceiling appeared.
Doctors shouting orders.
Masked faces leaning over him.
Sana’s voice trying to break through—
“Omar! Omar, I’m here! Don’t close your eyes!”

Everything started slipping.

His memories—
All seventeen years—
Rushed toward him in a single blinding wave:

Shanaya in school.
Majid’s laughter.
Hazir’s questions.
Coaching City.
Hyderabad nights on the platform.
The 12k salary.
Nuclear Technologies rising.
Sana in the parking lot.

Their first real conversation.
Their marriage.
Their children.
Every smile.
Every fear.
Every ache.
Every triumph.
Every quiet moment.

All of it collapsing into one final point.

A flash. A silence.

A soft falling inward. Black.

For a long moment, he existed without shape.

Then—

A warmth, A smell, A familiar rustle of steel plates.
The soft clang of a spoon against a tawa.

And a voice.

Not distant. Not muffled. Not imagined.

A voice he knew as deeply as breath itself.

"Omar... get up, beta. Here is your omelette and paratha."

His eyes snapped open. He inhaled sharply.

He was lying on the thin mattress in his small room in **AnuNagari**—the same room with the cracked wall, the dusty ceiling fan, the faded poster of a programming course he always meant to finish.

THE END

About the Author

Mohammad Kaif born 20 March 2005, young entrepreneur, writer, and creative technologist from India.
He is the **Founder & CEO of AtomProd**, a growing tech initiative focused on building innovative digital products and creative solutions for modern audiences.

Beyond entrepreneurship, Kaif is a passionate **Urdu poet**, blending emotion with precision in a style rooted in classical influence but shaped by contemporary thought. He is also a **writer**, **coder**, and **programmer**, committed to exploring how technology and storytelling can merge to create meaningful experiences.

The Life I Slept Into marks his entry into long-form fiction—a story inspired by dreams, identity, and untold inner lives. Kaif continues to build, write, and imagine new worlds across both technology and literature

www.ingramcontent.com/pod-product-compliance
Ingram Content Group UK Ltd.
Pitfield, Milton Keynes, MK11 3LW, UK
UKHW041344190726
13845UKWH00026B/428

9 789356 026148